SERENITY'S JOURNEY

Michelle,

I hope you enjoy my book.

C. L. Barrett

SERENITY'S JOURNEY

THE REUNION

C.L. BARRETT

Copyright © 2022 by C.L. Barrett.

Library of Congress Control Number:		2022907738
ISBN:	Hardcover	978-1-6698-2184-7
	Softcover	978-1-6698-2183-0
	eBook	978-1-6698-2182-3

All rights reserved. No part of this book may be reproduced or transmitted in any form or by any means, electronic or mechanical, including photocopying, recording, or by any information storage and retrieval system, without permission in writing from the copyright owner.

This is a work of fiction. Names, characters, places and incidents either are the product of the author's imagination or are used fictitiously, and any resemblance to any actual persons, living or dead, events, or locales is entirely coincidental.

Any people depicted in stock imagery provided by Getty Images are models, and such images are being used for illustrative purposes only.
Certain stock imagery © Getty Images.

Print information available on the last page.

Rev. date: 04/22/2022

To order additional copies of this book, contact:
Xlibris
844-714-8691
www.Xlibris.com
Orders@Xlibris.com
838156

GLOSSARY

dhampir. Half vampire and half human.

falcon. A race that is not known to humans, a race with many types of magic users.

feeder. A source of blood; mainly humans.

pureblood. One hundred percent vampire or human.

shape-shifter. A being that can take on human form along with one or more other forms.

VHs. Vampire hunters, humans or dhampirs who hunt vampires.

VHS. Vampire Hunter Society, a group that hunts vampires.

CHARACTERS

Serenity—Royal princess from a prominent Russian family. She uses many forms. She dresses mostly in black jeans, black sneakers, black trench coat; tank tops and shirts vary. Silver hair, silver eyes, fair skin.

Scott—Serenity's brother who is six months younger than her. He wears a black-and-green vest, a gray T-shirt, black-and-green jeans, black boots. Emerald-green eyes, tan skin; hair is green with silver highlights.

Prince Nightmare III—Also known as Nightmare III. He is a parental suiter for Serenity and heir to his father's lands. He has black hair, purple eyes, tan skin. He is normal dressed in royal attire of the Dragon family. He normally is in deep-purple kimono with a dragon print on the back and has two layers of attires.

Cloud—One of Serenity's protectors and traveling with Prince Nightmare III on his quest to find Serenity. Also a parental suiter to Serenity. He wears black and gray mostly, but if in Serenity's family lands, he dresses the part of protector and guard.

Exotic/Coalwind—A princess of Firelands in Japan. She has golden eyes, black long hair, tan skin. She rebels against her father, venturing away from the castle and capital lands. She wears gold dresses.

Yasha Vasiliev II—An archangel oracle. He is also an ally to Nikolai Belikov and his wife. His family is a sworn enemy of the Capulet family.

Janine—Green hair, green eyes, tan skin. Trained guardian. She is a dhampir. She is Scott and Serenity's mother.

Jonathan—Silver hair, silver eyes, fair skin. Lord of Capulet lands. Father to Scott and Serenity.

Charles—Head of royal guard in Capulet lands. He has light-green hair, light-blue eyes. He is a royal prince from anther land; he gave up his title to serve as Princess Serenity's guard and to direct the rest of the guards. His full title is Prince Charles Grincory. He was second prince in line back in his homeland.

Roza—Serenity's old friend and personal maid. She has red hair, pale skin, and red eyes. She attends to Princess Serenity's every need.

Lord Jason Hathaway—Lord of Hathaway lands in Japan. Brother to Janine Hathaway. Ally to Nikolai Belikov as much as possible without becoming a traitor to his brother-in-law.

Yasha Vasiliev I—Ally to Lord Belikov, father to Prince Yasha II. Title is Lord Vasiliev I. Light-green hair and light-blue eyes. Is an archangel with colorful wings but appears black to blend in.

Captain Mason—His full name is Lev Mason. He is the captain of the cruise ship that rescued Serenity and other cruise ship passengers and their captain, Jackson. He has red hair, red eyes, and tan skin. He grew up in Russia. He is a third-generation ship captain. The family has been loyal to the Belikov family for three generation, serving them when they want to travel by sea outside of Russia. Captain Mason is now supporting Serenity's journey.

Sasha—A wolf with a mix of red and blue fur.

Nikolai Belikov—An archangel that was trapped in crystal after defeated by Lord Capulet. He has silver hair, silver eyes, fair skin, and colorful wings; and his wings most of time appear black unless to another archangel. He appears to Serenity a spirit. He is also her biological father.

Irshrose Belikov—An archangel that was taken captive and hidden away by Lord Capulet. She has silver hair that turns blue halfway down when mated or during overuse of magic; she even gets markings of blue over her body. She has silver eyes, fair skin, and colorful wings like her mate. Her wings also appear black to anyone that is not an archangel.

General Siki—He trained Prince Nightmare III. He has black and gold hair, purple eyes, tan skin. He dressed in black and gold uniform with one gold and one black dragon facing each other with black behind the gold dragon and gold behind black dragon. The black and gold dragons facing each other is the royal crest of the royal

Dragon family. This crest is on all their uniforms worn by royal men and all members of the guard and military.

General Yuu—Long black hair, emerald-green eyes, tan skin; dressed in black and gold uniform with the royal crest of the royal Dragon family.

Nightmare II—Also known as Lord Dragon II. He is Nightmare III, Exotic, and Jade's father. He has purple eyes, long black hair, and tan skin. He's always seen in royal kimono with his family colors and royal symbol on it. He hates vampires.

Fang—He has short black hair, black eyes, tan skin, and black wings. He wears a trench coat that conceals his weapon. He is an old friend of Serenity's. He is also an enemy to Lord Capulet.

Head of Oracles—A man in charge of all oracles and wants control over the only oracle left in the Belikov family.

PROLOGUE

SCOTT IS SERENITY'S younger brother who was hiding in the Firelands of Japan. He ended up there after a trip to America went wrong and the family had to flee America. Scott has been in Japan for a month now, and within the first two weeks, he ran through all the money he brought with him; due to the fact he didn't know how to speak the langue, he couldn't get a job to have a source of money coming in to continue staying inside at night in a house over a cave in the woods. Scott didn't know how he would have survived if his family didn't help him get his weapons through airport security. But without it, he would have been in big trouble with wildlife and just trying to survive on the lands. He had training from the age of eight until he dropped out of school, not wanting the career path his family was trying to put him on a year before graduation. Scott loves his family but figured he could find better work than the low-paying job the private academy he was attending offered him. He didn't want to guard others from demons that are too hard to kill, for little pay.

This life-changing experience made him rethink what kind of career he wanted. Scott was thinking about everything while walking through the woods at night. Along his walk in the woods, Scott came upon a hot spring and noticed a woman swimming.

"Excuse me, miss, can I please join for a swim?" asked Scott.

"Yes, you may come in," said Coalwind.

He undressed until he was only in his boxers then stepped in to the hot spring and joined Coalwind. Coalwind and Scott were meeting for the first time; and both, not wanting to scare the other off, are keeping a secret from each other.

"Miss, could I please know your name?" asked Scott.

"My name is Coalwind, and may I know your name as well, sir?" asked Coalwind.

"My name is Scott, and it is nice to meet you, Coalwind," said Scott.

Coalwind and Scott were hanging out in the hot spring when out of nowhere, a dragon lands and shifts into human form. The man has long black hair, emerald-green eyes, tan skin, and is dressed in black and gold uniform with one gold and one black dragon facing each other, with black behind the gold dragon and gold behind the black dragon. The black and gold dragons facing each other is the royal crest of the royal Dragon family. This crest is on all their uniforms worn by royal men and all members of the guard and military. Scott didn't notice the man right off, unlike Coalwind. Scott noticed the man after Coalwind tensed up.

"Princess, what are you doing this far from the castle?" asked Yuu.

"I'm hanging out with my new friend Scott and to get away from home for a while," said Princess Coalwind.

"Your father is looking for you, princess, it is time to return home," said Yuu.

"Fine, give me a few minutes alone with my friend," said Princess Coalwind.

Yuu walked a few feet away to give the princess her privacy with her friend. Coalwind then turned her attention from Yuu, her father's general, to her friend Scott.

"Scott, I must go, but I'll find you later, and we can hang out again," said Coalwind.

Then Coalwind got out of the hot spring, got dressed, and walked away with Yuu before Scott could speak. Coalwind and Yuu switched forms and took to the sky one after the other. Coalwind went airborne first then Yuu. At this moment, Scott found out that Coalwind wasn't human and her secret that she was going to wait and tell him later. Scott was shocked at the sight of dragons in the skies; he couldn't believe what he was seeing. Also at that moment, he realized she was not human, but he didn't know exactly what she was. All Scott knew was that she was a dragon with a human form. Scott noticed day was breaking as he watched her flying way. Scott was wondering what he was going to do for food now that he was getting hungry and was going to need to sleep in a few hours. He needed to start heading back to the cave he'd been staying in the last few weeks. Scott was looking for prey on the way back to his cave.

Scott was wondering how the rest of his family were doing at the moment. He knew his sister would be on her way for him by now, he hoped, but his parents—he couldn't see them working unless they had to; they held themselves better than the people of their lands. Everyone in the family knew that Serenity was the one that the people wanted on the throne. She was kindhearted and always spending time among the people as an equal, not as a superior. Scott really didn't want to hunt for his meals anymore; he liked to have them made for him. He also knew his sister was lucky she could go without food if she wished. Scott was ready to be in a castle or a house, something that didn't have to be out in nature to shower and hunt from meal to meal. Scott was a bit envious of his sister; she had the ability to speak any langue and would be able to adapt and get a job and keep lodging, and she could manage money better than he ever could.

After an hour of hunting on the way back to the cave he'd been sleeping in and cooking his meals in, at the edge of the path back to his cave, he caught himself a dear. He skinned and cleaned it before taking the eatable meat back to the cave to cook it or dry it out to eat later as a snack. Scott thoughts went to how long it had been without seeing or hearing from his family. The promise they made back in America kept Scott from reaching out and trying to contact anyone in his family, even the family he has in Japan. He was leaving it up to Serenity to find him and reunite the family. Scott wondered if she even started looking for him or even had come to Japan yet. After finishing dinner and drying the rest of the meat, he went to bed without bathing. Scott was hoping he could see Princess Coalwind again tonight if it's convenient for her. Since she was a princess from this country.

FINDING SCOTT

CHAPTER ONE

IT IS DUSK in Japan. Serenity was just getting up for night traveling under the cover of darkness looking for her brother Scott. Scott was six months younger than Serenity and still irresponsible. Serenity was wondering if Scott blew through his money yet. It's been over month since Serenity had last seen her baby brother. She was wondering if the rest of her family were holding it in there while she was on a journey to reunite them all. She knew there still was a risk of her traveling in vampire form—even in Japan. There may be a bounty on her and her father after America. Her father recklessly fed in America and started this mass. Unlike her father, Serenity can take any form of her choosing. Her favorite form was a human bird known as a falcon. She has strong magic and was most controlled in this form.

Serenity had been walking around for three hours and spotted a bar and walked inside wearing black jeans, purple tank top, black jean jacket, and black sneakers. She has long silver hair, pale skin, and silver eyes. She was hoping she could find some information on her brother—maybe someone who had seen him or would recognize his description. She also would like to relax a bit. Serenity started mingling in a bar, and out of nowhere, trouble found her. Vampire Hunters walked into the bar and spotted her on the other side of the room near an exit. The hunters were off duty, so they were only two buddies going out for drinks, but they wanted the bounty on Serenity and her father. Serenity scanned the room and noticed the hunters walking toward her. She pushed through the exit and ran toward the woods to escape from the hunters. Once she hit the woods and was out of sight, she switched to a gray wolf and started running through the woods to lose the hunters.

The hunters that were chasing her noticed the sneaker prints disappeared in the woods. They looked round; all they saw were animal prints. The hunters wished they could track her by smell, but they couldn't; and if she was a shifter, picking up her track now would be impossible if she shifted. The hunters returned to their headquarters to file a report that Serenity Capulet had entered Japan and was suspected to be a shifter. They also inquired if the bounty was going up on her. The head hunter looked at them and gathered all hunters and ordered that Serenity Capulet was to be brought in alive.

***

Back in the forest, Serenity found herself wandering around to try finding a new exit from where she was and out of harm's way and also looking see if her brother Scott was living in the woods near her as well, but even in wolf form, she couldn't pick up his scent. Serenity continued wandering, and around dawn, she finally found an exit near a different bar that also had an inn attached to it. It was called Nighthowler.

Serenity walked in and up to the bar and ordered a strawberry-mango vodka mix on the rocks. The bartender handed her the drink but refused to take her money. She wanted to talk, but he put his hand over her lips and stared at her, leaving her speechless. Serenity was not liking the way the bartender was acting toward her; she grabbed his arm to remove it from her mouth. The night manager of the bar noticed Serenity grab his employee's hand and started walking toward the bar.

"Come on, miss, you know you like it," said the bartender.

"You know nothing, sir, keep your hands off me," said Serenity, angry.

The bartender grabbed her roughly and pulled her in close and kissed her roughly. The manager grabbed the bartender and pushed him away from Serenity.

"Renji, we do not touch our customers. Your behavior is out of line. Do I make myself clear?" said the manager.

Renji got very nervous when the manager started telling him what not to do and worried that later it would come up in the meeting in the manager's office and he'd get fired for laying a hand on a customer.

"Yes, sir, perfectly," said Renji.

"Miss, please come with me, I would like a word with you. And for the trouble the bartender caused, you may stay the night for free, and drinks are on the house," said the manager.

"Thank you, sir, and what can I help you with?" said Serenity.

"My name is Inten, and for starters, your name," said the manager.

"My name is Serenity, and what is it you really want to know?" asked Serenity, annoyed.

"If you are looking for someone?" asked Inten.

"Yes, I'm looking for my younger brother named Scott. Why do you want to know?" asked Serenity.

"What does he look like," asked Inten.

"Scott wears a black-and-green vest, a gray T-shirt, black-and-green jeans, black boots. Emerald-green eyes, tan skin; hair is green with silver highlights.

"He's been here before," said Inten.

"When, and how long ago was that?" asked Serenity.

"It has been two weeks now since I last seen him. He looked sad, like he was waiting to see someone," said Inten.

"It was probably me he was waiting for," said Serenity.

"Why, what happened to make him wait and not go looking for his family?" asked Inten.

"Sorry, I can't tell you that. I don't want it to endanger you or Nighthowler," said Serenity.

"Okay, I understand, Serenity, I won't pry any further," said Inten.

Serenity walked away after the two of them were done talking and headed get some sleep since it was daytime out now, and it was easier for her to travel by the cover of night but also a bit more dangerous. She lay in bed hungry but didn't want get up to get food. Serenity's hungry faded once she decided to take her natural form of a archangel. She should know better than to try to maintain a vampire form and avoid feeding like a vampire. She's forgotten the effects of taking other forms and still maintained her magic. After a few hours of rest, she woke and noticed it was still daytime out; and considering what she was trying to accomplish here in Japan, she couldn't travel during the daytime, so she rolled over and fell back to sleep knowing her goal.

CHAPTER TWO

CLOUD AND NIGHTMARE III woke up at the same time. Cloud was shocked to see Nightmare III up already and getting ready for the day.

"Nightmare III, you're up early, it is still light out, I thought you couldn't go out during the daytime," said Cloud.

"I can when I switch back to my main form or another form that can travel by day," said Nightmare III.

"What do you mean main form?" asked Cloud, surprised, learning something new about his travel companion.

"I'm a dragon shape-shifter, and it takes me a while to change back from vampire form after holding it so long," said Nightmare III.

"Why is it just coming now?" asked Cloud.

"Because I was in vampire form so long and was afraid no one would believe one truth about myself without proof," said Nightmare III.

"I can keep it from Serenity for now, but you better come clean to her next time you see her," said Cloud.

"Thank you, Cloud, I will," said Nightmare III.

After they finished their conversation, Cloud and Nightmare III took to the skies and started flying toward the Firelands. It was also Nightmare III's family land and place that Nightmare III thought would be a good home base to look for Serenity. While flying over the ocean, all they could think about was wondering if Serenity was safe and where she was currently at daytime.

It's around 11:00 p.m. when Cloud and Nightmare III touched down in a small village in Japan. The village was about a good four-hour flight to his family lands. They found a small inn in the village to stay for a few hours of rest. After they checked in to the inn, they went to see if they could find place to get a meal. Cloud and Nightmare III found a twenty-four-hour restaurant and got a table. Cloud hasn't been in Japan long enough yet to pick up the langue since he could adapt to the langue of any country he was in, so it was left to Nightmare III to order dinner for them.

The two of them ate in silence, not wanting to talk after a long flight to reach Japan. After dinner, they went back to the inn to get some rest. When they finally called it a night, it was around one o'clock in the morning.

CHAPTER THREE

COALWIND AND YUU landed just outside the castle gate and were about to enter when they were met by the gatekeepers.

"Let us pass. Lord Dragon II wishes to see Princess Coalwind in his chambers," said Head General Yuu.

"You both may pass," said the gatekeepers.

Coalwind was escorted to Lord Dragon II's meeting chambers. Head General Yuu knocked on the door.

"Come in," said Lord Dragon II from the other side of the door.

Yuu opened the door and let Coalwind into the throne room. She walked by him and up to the throne, where her father was seated to meet with others. Tonight, she was the only one in the room; it was only a decision for father and daughter.

"Father, I would like to change my name. I've hated the name Coalwind since I was old enough to understand the meaning of my name," said Coalwind.

"If that's what you wish, but let me tell you something I know since before you were hatched, then you can choose what name you want to change it to instead of Coalwind," said Lord Dragon II.

"Okay, I'll hear you out, Father," said Coalwind.

"It all happened many years ago while I was on a trip to a land far away from earth. It's a place where dragons lived freely and openly, and at the same time, their closest neighbors were vampires and archangels. For a long time the three kinds traded and lived in peace, but one day, both vampires and dragonkind ended up in civil war. Vampires were fighting their own kind, and dragons fighting their own. At the time, a young princess named Serenity was born to the archangel race, and her father was Nikolai. Nikolai, Serenity, Irshrose, Jonathan—all visited. When your father and mother were expecting to have children, Serenity was eighteen and had a vision of you and told them you wouldn't hatch until many years later. Shortly after that, war broke out. Serenity and her family who were archangels disappeared from the memories of everyone on Dragon Planet.

"I went to Dragon Planet because I was summoned there. Your real father handed me an egg and told me the child should be called Exotic Fireheart Dragon. I left there. As I did, a barrier went up in the lands, and the dragons that lived on Dragon Planet were forgotten. Some of them came to earth, and they now hide among humans. But the ones that couldn't take a human form were hunted down and eventually killed off. The point behind this story I tell you is that you should take your true name back if you want to change it, my daughter," said Lord Dragon.

"I want to change my first name back to *Exotic*, Father," said Coalwind.

"As you wish, sweetheart," said Lord Dragon II.

Exotic left her father excited to see Scott and tell him everything she learned, knowing her secret would be out now. She returned to her room to get some rest before sneaking out after dark to go see Scott.

CHAPTER FOUR

SERENITY GOT UP round 6:00 p.m. to get ready to leave the inn to go searching for her brother Scott. Serenity dressed in dark colors; she was wearing a navy-blue tank top, black jeans, and black sneakers, and she put on a black trench coat because it was misting outside, but she was not going let the weather stop her from continuing her search. She left the bar hoping the weather would pass since she was not in the mood to wear a coat. But she was going to wear it so she doesn't stand out as not being an actual person. She was walking in the woods figuring what would be the best way to find out if her brother had already run out of money. Serenity loved nature, so she was taking it all in while she was walking around looking for her brother Scott. She was taking all the sounds in the woods and all the sights to see.

After traveling most of the night and taking in the nature different from her homeland, she came upon a lava pool. Serenity decided to relax in the lava pool even though she should be looking for her brother. But to her, taking time to relax a bit is just as important as looking for Scott. Serenity has been swimming in the lava pool, not realizing an hour has already passed until a young royal guard approached her at the lava pool.

"Miss, what are you doing here?" demanded the royal guard.

"I was just swimming. Is there a problem with that?" asked Serenity.

"Yes, there is. This lava pool belongs to the Hathaway royal family here in Japan," said the royal guard.

"Well, I'm sorry. I will be on my way then," said Serenity.

She stepped out of the lava pool, got dried off, and dressed with magic to keep herself from being exposed to a guard of the royal family. She also wanted get out of there as fast as she could in case they decided to arrest her for trespassing on royal grounds not owned by her father. Let alone she didn't want to be recognized by any royal family at the moment. A member of the royal family approached Serenity and the royal guard. Serenity noticed him as the lord by the clothes he was wearing. She was thinking this could go bad really quick and wanted to run away but thought it may get worse if she decided to.

"Guard, stand down, she is family from Russia. She is full-blooded Russian like her father," said Lord Jason Hathaway.

"Yes, my lord," said the guard and went to survey the area for any threats.

"Princess Serenity Irshrose Capulet, why are you here in Japan, and why aren't your parents with you?" asked Lord Hathaway.

"We were attacked on our family vacation in America. We all went to different countries to hide, and I'm the one that has to reunite everyone. I'm here looking for my brother Scott," said Serenity.

"What can I do to help, my darling niece?" asked Hathaway.

"Have you seen my brother Scott, and do you have a place I can rest? I've been traveling by night to go undetected," asked Serenity.

"No, I haven't in a long time. What does he look like now? And yes, you can stay at my castle for as long as you need. Please stay few days to rest before going after your brother," said Lord Hathaway.

"Thank you very much, Uncle Jason. My brother has short green hair with silver highlights, tan skin, and emerald-green eyes," said Serenity.

Uncle Jason and Serenity were walking back to the castle together. His guard was with them and watched her as if she could be a danger to his lord. Only if the guard actually knew how much of a threat she could be to her uncle if he got on the wrong side of her, then he wouldn't just be watching, he would react before she became the threat. Uncle Jason and Serenity walked through the woods back to his castle; the walk took about an hour from the lava pool. When they returned to the castle, they were greeted by his butler.

"Welcome back, my lord," greeted the butler.

Jason turned his attention to his butler after being greeted.

"Please show my guest to a suitable room and make sure she has everything she needs and that all her needs are attended to. I'm retiring for the night," said Lord Hathaway.

"Yes, my lord, understood," said the butler.

"Miss, this way please," said the butler.

The butler led Serenity to a guest room as instructed by his lord. Two of the castle-guards decided to follow the new guest back to the room she would be staying in, even though the lord didn't give them orders to. One of the guards was a falcon and could sense the power that she holds and didn't want her to turn on his lord during his watch. They went down several hallways, and on the opposite side of the castle was where the lord's chambers were. The butler stopped in front of the bedroom door and opened it to let Serenity into her room.

"Miss, this is where you will be staying. I hope it is to your liking, and if there is anything you need, please just ask. There will be maids here to attend to your need," said the butler.

"Thank you, sir," said Serenity.

Then the butler saw himself out. As he left the room, the maids entered to check on their new guest.

"Miss, can we help you with anything?" asked one of the maids.

"No, I'm going to get some rest. You're dismissed," said Serenity.

The maids left the room so Serenity could rest for the rest of the day since it was near sunrise. Serenity prepared for bed in peace, switching from civilian clothes to nightgown. Serenity took one look at herself in a full-body mirror and remembered how much she didn't like dressing part of a royal or being in the presence of other royals. She lay in bed and fell asleep tired, but she didn't let her guard down being at her uncle's castle and in an unfamiliar country. Serenity slept peacefully until round noontime when she woke up because she was hungry for food. Since she was at her uncle's, she took the form she was more comfortable in, but it also didn't require blood to satisfy her hunger. She took her archangel form, which is with fair skin, silver hair with purple at the ends going halfway up her hair, looking like she dyed her hair. Her eyes were silver with purple in the middle due to magic. She didn't let her wings out in a vampire domain. She heard knocking on her door as she put on a bathrobe to go find dinner. She walked over to the door and answered it.

"Evening, Uncle Jason," said Serenity, being polite and acting friendly.

"Serenity, is there anything you need?" asked Uncle Jason.

"Yes, Uncle Jason, I need something to eat, I am hungry," said Serenity.

"Okay, follow me, I'll show you the way to the kitchen," said Uncle Jason.

Serenity followed him away from her guest room and down the hall. They came to a spot in middle off the hall, and one side of the hallway had a red door, and the other side of the hallway had big double doors. Uncle Jason looked at her before he spoke, "The red door is feeders, and the room across the ways is the dining hall. Both are open 24-7," said Uncle Jason.

"Thank you, Uncle Jason," said Serenity.

Serenity looked between the two trying to decide if she really wanted to blow what she was by actually eating real food, but she really didn't want to feed off of humans. She walked into the kitchen and ordered some food to eat and decided to worry about any consequences later. While she waited for dinner, she looked around the room and took in the beauty of the old-style castle. Serenity really wanted to explore the castle and know that she was unguarded at this time that she could get away with it on the way back to her guest room. Even though it was vampire night, she ordered a bunch of breakfast food. Serenity enjoyed her food and got up, walked out of the dining hall, and started to her guest room while taking in the beautiful surroundings in the castle. She made it back to her room with no trouble to find that there was a kitty on her guest bed. The kitty was black-and-white. Serenity sat on her bed and started to pat the kitty. After an hour, she fell asleep with the kitty curled up against her.

CHAPTER FIVE

SCOTT WAS JUST getting up; it was around 7:00 a.m., and he was hungry for some food after sleeping, but he knew it meant he would be going hunting for his meals. He knew waking up in a nice warm bed and a meal already prepared for him was a far-off dream since he was flat broke. Scott cleaned up his bedding and put it in a hiding compartment in the cave and walked out of the cave to go hunt and get breakfast for himself and some water to drink. He came up to a beautiful waterfall and, to his surprise, spotted Exotic under it; form the cliff looking round and found water below and the beautiful Exotic. He walked down a path that led down the cliff to the base of the pool and waterfall. When he reached the base of the pool, he got a better look at Exotic and noticed that she had nothing on, and he was trying to fight the urge to join her in the pool and under the waterfall. Exotic looked over her shoulder and saw Scott standing at the edge of the pool.

"Princess Coalwind, would you mind if I join you?" asked Scott.

"Scott, right, you can join me, and I need to tell you something important," said Exotic.

"What is it, Coalwind?" asked Scott, not knowing she illegally changed her name.

"I talked to my father and changed my name after finding out a bit about my past," said Exotic.

"What did you change it to?" asked Scott.

"I changed it to *Exotic*," said Exotic.

Scott stripped down until he was naked and joined her in the pool of water under the waterfall. Exotic and Scott enjoyed the water until early evening when it cooled off. Then they both got out of the water and dried off. Exotic looked at Scott with desire and passion. But neither acted on their feeling.

"Scott, I, Princess Exotic, extend you an invitation to stay at my family castle while you are here in Japan," said Princess Exotic.

"Thank you very much, Princess Exotic," said Scott with curtsy, bowing to the princess.

Since it was too late to make it to the Firelands castle, the two of them worked together to collect food and water. On the way back to the cave that Scott was using as a base camp, Scott started wondering what it would be like to actually have a girlfriend and able to return home safe and sound. Scott made sure the food they gathered was enough to feed them both. As they got back to the cave, he realized he may want to get more wood to keep them warm until morning.

"Exotic, I would hate to impose on you, but would you mind cooking while I gather more wood?" asked Scott.

"No, the fire is important too, go ahead, I'll have dinner done while you're gone," said Exotic.

Scott left the cave and went to gather wood in the surrounding area. Scott was wondering if his sister made it to Japan yet. Scott found dry wood really quick and was back to the cave within ten minutes, and he found Exotic still cooking dinner. He watched as she cooked up a bear he killed on the way back. Scott couldn't help but study Exotic's flawless body. She finished cooking dinner ten minutes later; they both ate, and Exotic cleaned up dinner, and Scott set up some things so they both could sleep comfortable and stay warm in a cool summer night. Scott made sure a fire was made before going to sleep himself.

The next morning, Exotic and Scott got up and went out and started heading through the woods toward Exotic's family lands, which was run by her father, Lord Dragon I. Scott packed up what he had and put it all in his backpack to carry with them to the Firelands. Scott knew everything he had would come in handy when he'd head back home with his sister once he was reunited with her. But it also provided for Exotic and him, if they have to stay another night in the woods. Exotic and Scott were walking through the woods. Exotic was leading the way to her family lands from the cave.

Scott was not letting his guard down in case they were attacked during their travels. Scott wanted to keep Exotic safe from any harm. They passed through one of the villages only four hours from her home and came across a restaurant at the edge of the village. Exotic started walking toward it hungry. Scott followed her hungry but knew he wouldn't eat, unable to afford food—broke. They sat at a table for two and started looking over the menu. Scott set down the menu, unable read or buy a meal and not saying a word to Exotic about both. Exotic looked up at him wondering why he set down the menu.

"Scott, why do you look so frustrated?" asked Exotic.

"I can't afford anything or even read the menu," said Scott, embarrassed now.

"It's fine. I'll order food and pick up the bill," said Exotic.

A waitress walked from across the restaurant to take their order.

"My princess, what can I get for you today?" asked the waitress.

"I'll have two eggs over easy, sausage links, and home fries. My companion will take scrambled eggs, two orders of sausage links, two orders of home fries, bacon, and a side of hash browns," said Princess Exotic.

"Okay, my princess, I'll put it right in," said the waitress.

The waitress left to put in their order without wasting time. Exotic and Scott waited in silence for the waitress to return with the food. Exotic decided to break the silence between Scott and her.

"Scott, I know you don't know the language here, but if you want, I can help you learn some of the basics," said Exotic.

"You sure? I wouldn't want to inconvenience you, princess," asked Scott.

"Yes, I'm sure, Scott, and you can pick up the rest as you go," said Exotic.

"Then teach me, princess," said Scott.

Exotic started teaching Scott the basics of Japanese. Before they knew it, the waitress has returned with their breakfast. The waitress set it down on the table based on their order.

"My princess, can I bring you anything else?" asked the waiter.

"No, thank you, we will be just fine," said Exotic.

Exotic and Scott took their time eating since they were in no rush make it back to her family lands. After finishing of their breakfast, Exotic paid the bill. Scott waited until she was ready leave before getting up. He was being a bit cautious recognizing the vampire hunters that had been after his sister. He was not sure if they would take in a dhampir like himself. He was not the one that did the killing back in America. Exotic noticed Scott watching two of the men that were sitting five tables away from them.

"Is there a problem?" asked Exotic.

"Not sure, those men are the same kind of guys after my father and sister and possibly me and my mother," said Scott.

"Just act normal, and it should draw no attention to us," said Exotic.

"Okay, you're right, everything should be fine," said Scott.

Exotic and Scott stood up and walked toward the exit. They were acting naturally in hopes not to draw the attention of the hunters. In case they got a brilliant idea to take one or both of them as hostages or worse. They got outside and in the clear, without the hunters deciding to follow them. They continued their adventure to the capital of Firelands. Exotic wondered if her father would take a liking to Scott or make him leave. She knew her father was very struck. But she wanted to be able to keep Scott around.

Alone, their walk turned from woods and villages to rocks and bricks once they entered the capital of Firelands. Scott was in awe at how amazing the capital was. All building work was of brick and brimstone. But the castle stood out of all. It was thirty stories high, and gems decorated the winds, doors, roof, and tower tops. The gate guarding the castle is made of stone. Exotic led Scott through the capital to the castle. Once they reached the gates, they were met by Yuu and a few other guards.

"My princess, your father wants see you now that you finally returned," said Yuu.

"As my father wishes, I'll go see him at once," said Exotic.

"Come, Scott, after I speak with my father, I'll show you to my corridors where you'll be staying," said Exotic.

"As you wish, princess," said Scott.

Exotic and Scott both walked past the guards with no trouble. The guards didn't have the authority turn away the princess and her guest. Little did they know he was another royal because he didn't dress the part. Exotic led the way to the throne room. She hated being summoned by her father but can't refuse his summons. They walked through several hallways that were just as amazing as the outside; lining windows with gems and crystals on board at the top of the hallway made it unique. Most castle doors were just wood. But throne doors had dragons on it, some out of gems. The dragon itself was done in one black onyx, and gold eyes and other gold with black onyx eyes. Scott stood to the side of the hall as Exotic knocked on the door. A guard opened it to see who it was then shut it to report it back to Lord Dragon I.

"My lord, Princess Exotic is here as you requested," said the guard.

"Show her in," demanded Lord Dragon II.

The guard opened the door and motioned Princess Exotic to enter the throne room. She walked in and up to the bottom step leading up to the royal throne.

"My lord, how may I assist?" asked Princess Exotic.

"Where has my daughter been wandering of to? And word reached me you brought a man home with you," demanded Lord Dragon I.

"My lord, I'm a seeker of knowledge of harvest lands, so I traveled away from the capital. In doing so, I made a new friend," said Princess Exotic.

"Tell me more of this friend," demanded Lord Dragon I.

"He is a foreigner to our country, and he's waiting for his sister to come and bring him home," said Princess Exotic.

"He can stay, you are dismissed," said Lord Dragon II.

Exotic turned and left her father without another word. She met Scott back outside the throne room. Without having to speak, Scott automatically followed Exotic to her corridors. Her living area and guest rooms were a hallway away from the throne room. Her private corridor consisted of five guest rooms and her big private room. She gave Scott the guest room two doors down from her private room. She walked away to prepare for dinner with her father that evening.

CHAPTER SIX

CLOUD AND NIGHTMARE woke up and got ready to make the last bit of journey to the Firelands this morning. Cloud's guard was up being that he was not sure if any enemies awaited them outside the inn or in the sky while they traveled. They left the inn after they made sure they had everything. Cloud and Nightmare III didn't get breakfast that morning; they wanted to get to the Firelands as quickly as possible. They walked to a clearing then spread their wings and took to the sky. Cloud and Nightmare III planned to fly nonstop to his family castle. The wind and sun were on their backs while they flew over nothing but lands and villages beneath them.

Cloud and Nightmare III both landed in the woods in a clearing a ways from the Firelands to make sure that they didn't get shot out of the sky by Nightmare III's family guards that guarded the castle from the rooftops. They were walking on foot the rest of the way to the castle. Walking through the village in civilian clothes after being away so long kept the land's people from recognizing their prince. Cloud took in the beauty of Nightmare III's family land's capital that went along with their lands. Once they reached the castle gate, they were stopped by guards. It was nightfall by the time they reached the castle. One of the guards at the gate directly answered to his father.

"My prince, Nightmare III, Lord Dragon II requests a meeting with you as soon as you have returned. And who is this with you?" asked the guard.

"Okay, I'll go to him at once. And his name is Cloud. We are looking for a friend that should be here somewhere in this country," said Prince Nightmare II.

"What is the name of this friend?" asked his father's guard.

"Her name is Serenity Irshrose Capulet," said Prince Nightmare III.

"Please follow me, my prince," said his father's guard.

Cloud and Nightmare III followed the guard to his father's chambers.

CHAPTER SEVEN

SERENITY WOKE UP around 3:00 p.m. She decided to get ready for the day. She started off by showering; she was not a big fan of bathing outside her home. She started by shampooing and conditioning her hair. She let the conditioner sit in her hair while she scrubbed her body clean from the night traveling. After she rinsed off her body and made sure the conditioner was out her hair, she turned off the water, then she reached out and grabbed tallow hanging up on a hook next to the shower. She dried off her left leg and foot first, stepped halfway out, then dried off her right leg and foot then stepped the rest of the way out of the shower. She walked back into her room that connected to the bathroom to dress for the day.

She decided to dress down from her royal attire because she was going out, not planning to stay in her uncle Jason's lands. She put on a baby pink tank top, her trench coat, a pair of black socks, and her black sneakers. She wanted to stay comfortable while traveling.

She was traveling through beautiful nature. It has tall trees that shaded the ground but let rays of sun come through on a good day. But today was overcast. Dark, damp, cloudy—it could start to rain any minute. In her travels through the woods, she came across a den just in time the sky opened up and she needed shelter from the storm. Since it's been overcast all day, Serenity didn't realize it was turning to night.

She had no choice but to check out the den and hole up in it until the weather passed. Serenity found a female wolf occupying the den to get out of the rain; unlike her, the wolf appeared to be just getting up where it was now turning to night. Serenity was guessing the wolf was female since she was all alone. The wolf went right to Serenity after she noticed her in the cave as well. The wolf started rubbing against Serenity like she wanted attention from her. Serenity kneeled down by the wolf and started patting her. The wolf had a mix of red and brown fur and eyes deep-blue like the ocean. Serenity noticed the storm had passed and went to stand up and leave the den to continue her search for her brother Scott. Serenity knew she couldn't stay with the wolf and befriend her any longer now that the weather had passed. Serenity walked to the entrance of the den, and the wolf followed her. The wolf did also notice that it was nice outside; she took her human form.

"Miss, why are you leaving now when I want play with you?" asked the wolf.

"I need to find my brother," said Serenity.

"How is it that you have a human form?" asked Serenity, surprised by what she saw the girl do.

"Most of us wolves have the ability to appear human and communicate with humans but choose not to," said the wolf.

"If you would like to join me in my travels, you can," said Serenity, inviting the wolf to join her for company.

Serenity was starting to feel lonely without a travel companion. The wolf decided to join Serenity on her journey without any hesitation.

"I have a name. It's Sasha," said the wolf.

"Nice to meet you, Sasha, and mine is Serenity," said Serenity.

Serenity couldn't help but think how cute it was that Sasha had ears and a tail in her human form. Sasha's ears and tail were a reddish brown; her eyes were still a deep ocean blue, along with a tan skin. She wore a black leather vest with spikes and studs on them that unzipped, showing off a dark-purple tank top. She also wore black leather jeans that had chains dangling off them, crossing in the back, a leather belt with a chain clipped to it and attached to a holster at her hip holding her handgun. Sasha and Serenity started traveling together through the woods to see if they can find a village to get some food; both of them were getting hungry for something to eat. They had been walking awhile to get out of the woods and came upon a small village. They were searching for a place get some dinner and spotted a restaurant at the edge of the village and went in to get dinner and sat down at a table for two. The waiter walked over to the table and noticed that two creatures walked into the restaurant.

"Silver-haired girl, what is your kind doing here? We don't serve vampires and their pets," said the waiter.

Sasha stood up, not thinking, and pulled out her gun and pointed it at the waiter.

"You human, where is the sign that says you can't serve my friend or me?" demanded Sasha.

"We don't have one, it just is an unspoken rule," said the waiter.

Serenity stood up and put her hand over Sasha's, forcing Sasha to point her gun down at the floor way from the waiter.

"Sasha, let me handle this before it gets too out of hand, and no killing just because you're angry at the waiter," said Serenity.

"Okay, Serenity, you're right. I went too far because I'm overprotective of my friends," said Sasha.

"Waiter, bring me your boss now," demanded Serenity.

"If not, you'll have to deal with my temper, which I grantee is more deadly and won't leave a trace," threatened Serenity in the same breath as her demand.

"Fine, miss, but he will mostly give you the same answer I just did," said the waiter.

The waiter left walking across the restaurant, scared shitless between the girls' behavior but wouldn't allow it to show on his face. The waiter didn't want be teased or called a sissy by his coworkers.

Serenity started to get impatient because ten minutes passed before she noticed both the waiter and a much-more-built man walking back to the table that Sasha and she were sitting at. The waiter was hoping the girls had left the restaurant already, since he took his time to get his boss. But as he and his boss approached the table, the waiter was dumbfounded seeing the girls still sitting there.

"Sir, can I assume you are the manager of this restaurant?" asked Serenity.

"Yes, how can I help you this evening, miss?" asked the manager.

"My friend and I would like to eat dinner here, but your waiter refused to serve us," said Serenity.

"What would you ladies like for dinner tonight? I'll take your order, and it'll be on the house tonight," said the manager.

"Thank you, sir, we would like our two hot dogs and fries as a meal for my friend, and I would like your turkey sandwich," said Serenity.

The manager left with the waiter after taking their order. The manager turned to the waiter after dropping off the order to cook.

"My office now," said the manager.

"Yes, boss," said the waiter.

The manager knew he had some time before the customers' meals were ready, and he wanted to deal with the waiter that had treated the customers poorly.

"Do you know why I called you into my office tonight?" asked the manager.

"No. Why, boss?" asked the waiter.

"You shouldn't have handled the situation the way you did, refusing service because they are not human is poor customer service skills," said the manager.

"So, what does that mean for my job?" asked the waiter.

"Consider this as your only warning, and you get the rest of the night off unpaid," said the manager.

Back at the table, while Sasha and Serenity waited for dinner, Sasha looked up at Serenity before talking.

"Serenity, how did you handle that without killing that waiter for his rudeness?" asked Sasha.

"It was because I spent a lot of time round my older brother Jonathan. He taught me how to handle tough situations without resorting to violence," said Serenity.

Serenity remembered how much she missed her big brother. Sasha, unable to respond or come up with another question or subject to talk about, let it slip to silence while they waited for their meals. A few minutes later, the manager returned with their meals.

"Sorry for the wait, hope you enjoy your meal, and you're free to leave after you have finished your meal—it is on the house," said the manager.

"Thank you. Sorry for the *scene* we caused," said Serenity.

"No, no, it is I who should be the one to apologize for my worker's behavior," said the manager.

He left the ladies to eat their dinner in peace. Sasha and Serenity started talking about what they liked and disliked and starting to get to know each other better. They didn't realize they were quickly becoming friends.

CHAPTER EIGHT

CLOUD AND NIGHTMARE III reached the chambers of Lord Dragon II swiftly and quickly with Yuu as their guide. Nightmare III turned to Cloud then spoke, "Cloud, please wait out here while I speak with my father," asked Prince Nightmare III.

"Okay, I'll be right here when you are done," said Cloud.

Prince Nightmare III knocked on the throne room door, not wanting to disobey his father and barge into the throne room. A guard opened the door to see who it was then turned to his lord to report it.

"My lord, Prince Nightmare III wishes an audience with you," said the guard.

"Let him in," replied Lord Dragon II.

The guard opened the door to allow Prince Nightmare III to enter the throne room. Prince Nightmare III walked in to face his father, the lord, without second thoughts, knowing talking to his father didn't mean he was in any trouble.

"My lord, you wished to see me," said Prince Nightmare III.

"Yes, Prince Nightmare III, what brings my son home from his grandparents in Scotland?" asked Lord Dragon II.

"My companion and I are looking for a friend who came to this country, my lord," said Prince Nightmare III.

"We will discuss this further after dinner. You are excused to prepare for dinner," said Lord Dragon II.

"Yes, my lord," said Prince Nightmare III.

Prince Nightmare III turned away from Lord Nightmare II to leave since he was dismissed until after dinner. Prince Nightmare III went to go meet up with Cloud. Once he walked outside the throne room, Cloud followed Prince Nightmare III down the hallway. Price Nightmare III started leading Cloud toward his private chambers. All the princes and princesses had their private chambers with guest rooms for their guests. Prince Nightmare III's corridors were on the other side of the castle compared to the throne room on the south side and his corridors on the northern side of the castle. So they walked around the dining hall to get back to his corridors. Like his sister, he had five guest rooms as well. Prince Nightmare III gave Cloud one that was the second door from his room, but in between Cloud's guest room and Prince Nightmare III's room was his private study. It was also a place he planned to help Cloud plan to find Serenity after dinner. For now, Prince Nightmare III had Cloud retire to his guest room and prepare for dinner in proper attire.

CHAPTER NINE

EXOTIC WAS IN her bedroom preparing for dinner, but not wanting to because it meant dressing the part of the royal family in a fancy dress and wearing the crown. Out of all her dresses, she picked one that was a gold and black kimono that had red flowers on the front, and the dress went down to the floor; it was a traditional dress. It one of dresses her father had brought her to wear durn balls or family dinners. The clothes she wore among the people or when traveling, she had to buy herself. She left her hair down, being a bit rebellious this evening, heating it up. She walked out her room to meet Scott.

Scott was in his guest room and looking for something to wear since the servants took his only set of clothes to wash it. Scott decided to look in the closet. He found men's attire. He wasn't sure whom they belonged to, but at this point, he didn't have much choice but to dress in them. They were to dress in the Russian custom for royals. Royal uniforms to his royal house. But he was not sure how her family got their hands on it. He tried one on to see if it would fit him. It was a black-and-red uninform with a white rose on the left-hand side. The top button-down front went over red-and-black dress pants. He threw on men's dress shoes, and not to disgrace his family, he had a clean shave and got his hair cut short so it would look good and not like he hasn't kept up his appearance in months. After he was ready, he met Exotic outside their rooms.

Exotic looked at Scott all freshly dressed and was shocked at the meager difference with a clean shave and haircut. Scott noticed shock in her eyes and decided to speak to her.

"Princess Exotic, does this change scare you?" asked Scott.

"No, no, it makes you look more handsome," said Exotic.

"Well, you're just as lovely in your dress. It complements your eyes beautifully," said Scott.

"Thank you, Scott," said Exotic, embarrassed to be dressed as a royal and blushed.

"If you're ready, princess, we should meet the others for the dining hall," said Scott.

"Yes, let's go," said Exotic.

They walked together to the south entrance of the dining hall.

***

Prince Nightmare III opened up the doors to his closet and grabbed out one of his royal kimonos. It was a black top and bottom (with his custom gold kimono coat with the royal dragon family crest on the back of it) with men's traditional footwear. He then made sure he was suitable for dinner with his family before meeting Cloud, his guest, in the hallway. He walked out of his room when he was sure he was ready to face his father and mother.

Cloud found himself in a predicament; the servants came and took his only set of clothes, saying they needed to be cleaned and were not appropriate for dinner. Cloud, in just his boxers, opened a closet hoping that they may have something suitable for a Russian guard to wear. To his much grateful surprise, there was the standard-issue button-down black top and bottoms, along with standard guard boots sitting under the uniform. The top guard top did have a rose on the left arm. It also had his name on the right side and his rank on the left side. He wondered if this was friendly (gesture) or a way to declare he was a prisoner to this country or royal family. When Cloud was ready and still a bit nervous of the meaning behind why he had a Russian uniform here, he went to meet Prince Nightmare III in the hallway.

Prince Nightmare III was a bit surprised see Cloud dressed nicely for dinner and was not sure of the meaning behind it, so he decided to talk with his friend. Cloud also noticed Prince Nightmare III was just as surprised as he about this.

"Cloud, why are you dressed so nicely? We didn't travel with any of our prepared attires," asked Prince Nightmare III.

"I'm not sure myself," said Cloud.

"We will have to speak with Lord Dragon II on this later then," said Prince Nightmare III.

"Agreed," said Cloud. "Shall we head to the dining hall then, Prince Nightmare III?" asked Cloud.

"Yes, let's," said Prince Nightmare III.

They walked to the north entrance to the dining hall at the end of the hallway.

CHAPTER TEN

LORD DRAGON II and Lady Paradise were in their chambers preparing for dinner as well. Lord Dragon II put on one of his kimonos. His was gray top and bottoms. He also put on his teal kimono coat with a gray dragon on the back and on the left chest side and left arm. Lady Paradise put on a teal kimono with violet flowers all over it. Lady Paradise had shoulder-length blond hair, black eyes, and fair skin. Lord Dragon II looked to his wife and lady, taking in how gorgeous she was, before addressing her.

"My lady, shall we head to dinner to join our lovely children and their guests?" asked Lord Dragon II.

"Yes, my lord," said Lady Paradise.

They walked out of the room together and down to the dining hall. Their chambers were on the west side of the castle. Everyone entered the dining hall all at the same time from the entrance connected to their hallway. The lord went to the head of the table with his lady. The lady sat left to lord at the head of the table. Princess Exotic and her guest sat on the left side as well, and Prince Nightmare III and his guest sat on the right side; the heir to the throne sat to the right of the lord at the head of table as well. Lord Dragon II stood up and addressed his children.

"Exotic and Nightmare III, please introduce your guest to the family," said Lord Dragon than sat back down.

"Yes, Father," replied Nightmare III.

"Yes, Daddy," replied Exotic.

Nightmare III started, being the heir.

"Father, Mother, and sister, this is my friend Cloud, he is a falcon," said Nightmare III, choosing his words very carefully.

"Daddy, Mother, and brother, this is my friend Scott, and he's a dhampir," said Exotic, also choosing her words carefully.

Cloud was discreetly checking Scott's appearance and uniform, recognizing it as Capulet's royal house.

"Please tell us more about your friends," said Nightmare II.

"Cloud traveled here with me to help me find our friend Serenity, who's looking for her brother Scott," said Nightmare III.

"Scott had been hiding out in one of caves after going through what little money he had. Also, the language barrier has kept him from getting a job and stay in any type of lodging. He has been living off the land for food and shelter for the past few weeks, that I'm aware of," said Exotic.

"Well, I think the best approach to this will be having our men look for Scott's sister, if she's still here in Japan," said Dragon II.

"Scott, do you believe your sister is still here in our country?" asked Lord Dragon II.

"Yes, Lord Dragon II, she wouldn't leave without knowing if I'm dead or alive and bring me home if she can," replied Scott honestly.

"We can help you find her, but there is a catch. If she's in Lord Hathaway's lands, we can't touch her or go there," said Lord Dragon II.

"Please help find my sister, Lord Dragon II," pleaded Scott.

"I will. It may take few a days to locate her, and if we find out she's on the Hathaway lands, we will request for her presence here in Firelands. It's the best I can offer," said Lord Dragon II.

"Okay, thank you, Lord Dragon II," said Scott.

Then they finished dinner in silence and retired back to their rooms for the evening. Scott and Cloud both stayed in a hall after the rest of the parties retired for the evening.

"Cloud, what is your plans with my sister?" asked Scott, suspicious of Cloud's intentions toward Serenity.

"As of right now only find her and protect her nothing more," said Cloud honestly.

Scott didn't like the answer but thought better of pushing it any further due to the fact that falcon help is always useful in times of battle. He dropped the subject and walked away, returning to his corridors in the south wing. Cloud didn't go after the young prince; instead, he returned to his corridors in the north wing. Both went their separate ways.

CHAPTER ELEVEN

SASHA AND SERENITY kept on traveling after getting done at the restaurant because it was still a few hours before dawn. They both wanted to cover as much ground as they can before first light. Sasha and Serenity found themselves in a dark part of the woods; out of nowhere, another demon jumped out at them. Since Serenity has night vision, she could tell the man before her was 7'4" tall, of muscular build, and has black hair, light-blue eyes, and fair skin. He was wearing black leather pants with chains, a black T-shirt, customized back trench coat to hold all his weapons. He also wore a spiked and studded leather choker, studded leather bracelets on his right wrist, and a cross with red gems on it in four points and one in the middle.

"What are you ladies doing tonight?" asked the stranger.

"Who hell are you to try come on to us?" asked Sasha.

"Hey, Serenity, can you back down that cat? She is quite tempered," asked the stranger.

"Why should I, Fang? It's been two years since you last visited me, and she is a wolf, not a cat," demanded Serenity.

"Because we both know I am useful when it comes to fighting vampire hunters or other dangers," said Fang.

"Fine, Fang, but I won't make her stop watching you while you're with us," said Serenity.

Fang joined the group, not arguing over whether it was necessary that the wolf was watching him. They were very close to the Firelands at this point. Serenity didn't know it yet, but Scott was somewhere in the lands they were about to cross into. Suddenly a large group from the Vampire Hunter Society showed up out of the middle of nowhere. Serenity and her companions didn't even sense or hear them ahead of time. Sasha and Fang grabbed their weapons while Serenity used her magic to create blood whips on each of her hands. Serenity couldn't use her favorite weapon around her companions. She has never worked in a team before with Sasha or Fang. She was hungry and tired at this point. It was almost dawn as well. They all knew the fighting could last for hours against a countless number of hunters.

Fang, Sasha, and Serenity formed a triangle to try and fight their enemy. Serenity realized blood whips wouldn't work a few minutes and tried casting a very powerful spell while low on energy and collapsed when the spell failed. The hunters pushed their advance harder now with her down. Sasha turned to Serenity, concerned for her safety. Fang noticed Serenity was down and that he needed to put an end to this fight ASAP. Fang grabbed his secret weapon out that only Serenity knew what it does. The weapon was small, looked like a .49-caliber hand gun. Serenity looked up at Sasha with a serious face.

"We have to go now," demanded Serenity urgently.

"Why, Serenity?" asked Sasha.

"Explain later. We need to go now," demanded Serenity.

"Fine," said Sasha.

Serenity grabbed Sasha and jumped toward the sky, surprising everyone. She spread her wings, took off quickly, and raised altitude quickly until she was too high for the hunters to see them. While the hunters processed what just happened, it took Serenity twenty seconds to pull off a daring and narrow escape. She used a gift passed down from her father, the ability to use wings in any form she takes.

Serenity started flying back to her uncle's castle for safety. When suddenly five of her uncle's guards surrounded them in the air. Two grabbed the wolf girl, and one grabbed Serenity through a cape over her fair skin to keep her protected from the sun while in a weakened state. Sasha started getting feisty and fighting the royal guard, not knowing why they have a hold of Serenity, or she forgetting they weren't on the ground anymore, in just as much shock over Serenity's actions as the hunters'.

"Miss, calm down, we aren't going to harm you at the moment, and we won't harm Princess Serenity," urged the guard.

"What about me?" demanded Sasha.

"That decision rests solely with Lord Hathaway when we return back to his castle. And where is Fang? I can tell he was with you," said the guard.

"We left him behind. Actually Serenity made the call, the rest is a blur to me until you guys showed up," said Sasha.

Few minutes later, after flying the rest of the way in silence, they landed in front of the castle. They were met by other guards, and Sasha was arrested immediately upon the guards touching down with her. They also stripped her of her weapons she was carrying on her. Three guards escorted the prisoner to Lord Hathaway's throne room. The remaining two took Serenity to the guest room and were instructed to keep guard until the next shift comes in.

CHAPTER TWELVE

A PATROL GUARD SAW the battle outside the gate of the Firelands and recognized the description of the young woman that was Scott's sister. He was instructed in locating her, not assisting her. So he watched to see how the battle played out, and he couldn't tell what the weapon was that the man used, but it was deadly. He also watched from a safe distance to see Lord Hathaway's guards take her and a wolf girl into custody in the air, so he couldn't approach her to ask her to join him at the castle to speak with Lord Dragon II. He immediately returned to the castle, running through the villages and the capital. He also ran through the castle to the throne room, without knocking on the door; he barged in to report his findings to Lord Dragon II.

"My lord, I bring urgent news on the Capulet girl," said the guard, speaking fast so his lord wouldn't kill him for not knocking on the door, following protocol.

"Speak," demanded Lord Dragon II.

"Serenity has been found, but she was with the Hathaway royal guard, five of them returning back to the Hathaway castle after a battle with hunters," said the guard.

"Dismissed," ordered Lord Dragon II.

Lord Dragon II left the throne room as well, walking toward his daughter's private wing to speak with Scott since the matter was related to his sister. He also didn't want his son to get reckless and try barging in to the Hathaway lands and castle. Lord Dragon II knocked on the door to Scott's room out of respect of the early hour, not wanting to intrude on him if he was asleep. Scott heard the door and rushed to it to see who it was at this ungodly hour. Being that very early in the morning and most of castle asleep, he opened the door see that it was Lord Dragon II himself. He stepped aside to allow Lord Dragon II in to his guestroom.

"Lord Dragon II, can I help you?" asked Scott.

"I bring news of your sister, but it doesn't leave this room, understand?" asked Lord Dragon II.

"Yes, Lord Dragon II, I understand. Please tell me what you know," asked Scott.

"We have found out that your sister is at Lord Hathaway's castle, but I can't guarantee her or her companions will be safe there. I also can't interfere with other royal families' affairs," said Lord Dragon II.

"If you're okay with it, I would like to stay here and wait instead of going to Lord Hathaway's castle," asked Scott.

"You're more than welcome to stay here while waiting for your sister. Besides, I would like to meet the woman that stole my son's heart," said Lord Dragon II.

"Thank you very much, Lord Dragon II," said Scott.

Scott saw Lord Dragon II to the door and let him out after they were done talking. Scott returned to his bed more restless, wondering how his uncle will treat Serenity; he never cared for her in the very few times they visited, but politics kept it friendly. Scott finally fell asleep around dawn, being he was exhausted.

CHAPTER THIRTEEN

THE GUARDS ENTERED the throne room with the prisoner. Sasha opened her eyes, and by what she could tell, it was Lord Hathaway standing before her.

"Lord Hathaway, please, I'm a friend of Serenity," begged Sasha.

"Why would my niece be friends with a demon dressed like you? The way she dresses is bad enough when she's not with her family," said Lord Hathaway.

"Because she likes hanging out with me, she doesn't care how I dress," said Sasha.

Lord Hathaway reluctantly let Sasha go but was having his guards watch her while she remained in the castle, not trusting a wolf more than his niece. Sasha left the throne room unsure if she was still a prisoner or free to go where she pleased. Sasha wandered the castle trying to pick up Serenity's scent but had no luck until she came to the guest hall and spotted guards in front of a room. She realized it to be Serenity's—sure, her uncle wouldn't leave her unguarded in the castle. The guards let her in Serenity's room; they figured it was better to watch them while they were together than separated in the castle. Sasha saw Serenity sound asleep and switched to wolf form and curled up beside Serenity and fell asleep soundly.

Serenity was up early dawn, round four o'clock. Serenity was walking into the guest bathroom and found a warm bath already drawn up for her.

She took off her nightwear and stepped into the warm bath and relaxed while she got cleaned up for the day. Serenity wondered how Fang was doing since she took Sasha and fled the battlefield. She didn't dwell on it since her focus was finding her brother. After about thirty minutes in the tub, she got out wrapped up in a towel and walked back into her guest room. She decided to use magic to dress herself and dry her hair. She put on dark colors and a cape that was provided by her uncle; she adjusted with magic to cloak her so she can't be seen and invisible to everyone. She wanted to move about unguarded. She left leaving the cloak off to go get food in the dining hall. She refused to feed like her Uncle Jason and the rest of her family. She felt so out of place among vampires when they feed. She walked to the dining hall in the guest quarters to avoid speaking with her uncle if he was up. But she was grateful that her uncle was letting her stay here. She ordered a big breakfast to recover the magic she used up, and food always was the best way to recover magic. When the food was brought to her, Serenity started wolfing it down, starving. To eat a large meal, it only took her ten minutes. After, she walked from the dining hall to leave the castle; heading toward the main entrance, once she spotted a guard, she slipped on the cloak to get out the castle undetected. She started back toward the Firelands knowing she will end up meeting up with Fang again. She could use the safety that comes from having him around on her journey to find her brother Scott.

CHAPTER FOURTEEN

FANG ESCAPED BEFORE any of the nearby guards from the board of the Firelands spotted him or the fact he just massacred over one hundred vampire hunters so Serenity and Sasha could escape with their lives as well. He retreated to the hotel he has been using as a hideout from his royal family back in Russia. He went to the room he's been staying in and went straight to the bathroom to clean up; he had gotten blood splattered all over himself. Also as a consequence of his action, his magic marked his skin in dark purple marks all over his skin; the design of the markings is unique to each falcon shifter. He took a hot relaxing shower, knowing it was his day out and he's better off meeting up with Serenity after nightfall. Fang was trying to wash away the magic from his skin, the proof of his sin of taking another life. Fang didn't regret what he did; it was all in the name of protecting a princess he cares for while they both were far away from home.

Fang got out of the shower and put on boxers to get some rest before nightfall; he knew it would help dull the magic on his skin. His hope was that it would at least fade away from his face and neck; the rest of his skin, he could cover up with clothes and gloves. Fang's sleep was not a peaceful one; he fell into a nightmare as soon as he fell into a deep sleep. He was thrown into a scene that scared him to death—his worst nightmare. Serenity and he were seen together by both their parents. A fight broke out between the royal families, and her parents were killed, and as her father's guard went for Fang with a blade covered in magic, he woke up. This nightmare has haunted him for many years ever since the fallout between the royal families when they were only ten years old during a royal ball. Fang turned over, looked at clock, shaking as always from that nightmare, and realized he needed to get ready to leave. He dressed quickly and went into the bathroom and looked in the mirror to see how much magic was on his skin. He noticed it faded to pale purple, barely noticeable. He knew that Serenity can notice the marking from his magic since she was a royal archangel shape-shifter living with a family of vampires and dhampirs. She never let them see her true self. The one he's seen many times. He walked in his room to make sure he was not leaving any weapons he may need for his journey; he wanted to continue with Serenity and leave to meet her halfway between her uncle Jason's castle and the Firelands.

***

Fang and Serenity met up, and Fang wanted to talk to Serenity alone before Sasha got a chance to catch up to her.

"Princess Serenity, please, we need to talk before Sasha catches up," said Fang.

"Okay, Fang, we can go somewhere a bit more private," Serenity said, having the perfect place in mind.

"Yes, Princess Serenity, I'll follow you," said Fang.

Serenity led the way to a place she liked to go to get questions answered and replenish herself. But she knew that Fang won't know where they were, but for her, it was for her comfort and safety in Japan. Serenity and Fang entered an ancient underground temple. Serenity remembered her father's warning her to stay away from temples and anything related to the past but never understood why.

"Fang, if you are worried about your secret getting out to Sasha, that is not mine to tell for now, she is in the dark. That secret is yours to tell her about your powers that protected her and me in the battle that we all were lucky to escape from with our lives," said Serenity.

"Yes, I understand, Princess Serenity," said Fang.

Serenity walked deeper into the temple, forgetting why her father warned her away from them. Serenity wanted to explore the depths of the temple and speak to the gods and oracles, not knowing why she was being pulled in, feeling she needed to know something that the temple offered her. Fang tried to follow, but it was as if an invisible wall came up between him and the princess; he ran for the exit, hoping his presence gone from the temple will have her turn back and leave as well.

He feared what will become of her if she went deeper in to the depths of the temple.

Fang knew her family ties to gods and oracles and didn't want it to trap her here in this temple. Fang knew she was tied to darkness even if she didn't see it yet. Fang wished he could save her from her fate.

CHAPTER FIFTEEN

SASHA WAS JUST waking up back in Serenity's guest room in Lord Hathaway's castle. Sasha quickly realized that Serenity was not in bed with her; she looked out the window and realized it was also past dusk. She looked down on the bed and noticed a cloak and a note addressed to her. Sasha couldn't read, so she picked up the note and burned it so no one would know what it said. She knew it must be her way out of the castle. Sasha went to the dining hall, got a quick breakfast, and then started toward the castle's main entrance, a cloak lying over one arm until she needed to throw it on to exit the castle unseen. She sensed there were a lot of guards up head near the main hallway, so she threw on the cloak that Serenity left her. She walked on one side of the hallway, as close to the wall as possible, to avoid the guards; and when she came to guards in standing position on one side of the hall, she went around them. Sasha knew that the guards will throw her in the dungeon if she got caught outside of Serenity's room alone. She was clever and sneaked out with a couple leaving the castle; since the doors were closed unless people were coming or going from the castle. Sasha stuck close to a group leaving to make sure she can get outside the castle safely. When she made it outside safely, she headed back toward the Firelands knowing that is where Serenity would have headed after leaving her uncle's castle. For now, Sasha kept her cloak on so she can go undetected while meeting back up with Serenity. She hoped that Fang doesn't rejoin the group; she was not fond of him around Serenity. She traveled through lord Hathaway's lands covered in the cloak so his guards won't see her and drag her back to the castle for questioning of Serenity's whereabouts.

Sasha took her cloak off after she reached the forest just outside the Hathaway lands. Then she started running to catch up with Serenity, knowing that Serenity had to have left just before dusk. Sasha met up with Fang outside the temple and looked around, panicked that Serenity was not anywhere in sight. Sasha started howling to try to locate Serenity or get her to come back to them.

CHAPTER SIXTEEN

SERENITY LOOKED BEHIND her and noticed Fang was not there and heard Sasha's howl from a distance. She was wondering if she should turn back. She knew in her heart that she needed to go forward, but her father's warning came to mind, begging her to turn back before sinking into the darkness that he's been trying to protect her from. As she went to turn back, a spirit appeared before her. The spirit was strong and started forcing her to face the darkness, but she also remembered light that was dim within her and called it out to light up the room. She than realized it was too late to leave the temple now that she was in the center that called forth oracles and gods. Serenity worried what she'd gotten into being in the center of the temple. Everything around her changed; golden temple instead became mist, cloud, and silver halls were lined with doors of gold. It was like she stepped into one of her dreams. A man with silver hair appeared before her.

"Serenity, you have been summoned here. We need you to fulfill your role as oracle after your father. Your ties to darkness are what called you to us as an oracle of death," said the silver-haired man.

"I'm sorry, but I cannot become the next family oracle at the moment. I have to reunite my family," said Serenity.

"You are a child gifted with the power of a goddess, and you're refusing this calling?" asked the silver-haired man, confused.

"I'm my father's only heir. I will not let my family lands fall into ruin to become an oracle or goddess at this time," said Serenity.

"Stubborn child as always, but you will one day come to your calling, but for now, return to the world of humans," said the silver-haired man.

A world faded from misty halls to golden temples. When she realized she was back in the temple, she looked toward its exit and whispered, "Father, please forgive me for not heeding your warnings from when I was a child." As she went to leave the temple, another spirit appeared before her; this time, she recognized him. This time it was her father. She collapsed to her knees realizing the truth her father was really gone and dead.

"My daughter, you're strong. Rise and leave these temples and don't look back. You know what you must do. Follow your heart and keep the promise you made to the family you have," said her father.

"Yes, Father, as you wish," said Serenity.

Serenity stood up, noticed her father's spirit had gone, and she ran for the exit, crying, missing her father and the life she once knew long ago. Knowing she can't change the past and her father's death, all she can do is find out the truth. Serenity hated sleeping; most of the time her dreams were actually nightmares of the past. Serenity reached the exit, looked back hoping to see her father's spirit once more; and when he didn't appear, she stepped outside the temple to see her friends waiting for her. She was shocked to see Sasha howling and Fang pacing, panicked since they couldn't reach her in the temple. Serenity ran up to her friends about to say something when both noticed her and hugged her, relieved to see her safe.

"Fang and Sasha, nice to see you guys, are you both ready to head back to the Firelands? I'm safe," said Serenity.

"As you wish, Serenity," said Fang and Sasha.

Since the temple was in a big enough clearing, Serenity got a running start and took to the sky. Fang followed her lead. As for Sasha, she started to run under Serenity and Fang. Sasha was their eyes on the ground even though Fang and Serenity could see ahead of them from the sky. Sasha could see if anyone came up on them from the ground, if they were cloaking themselves in magic, to stay out of detection from anyone with the ability to sense them from the sky.

Fang and Serenity crossed in to the Firelands by air and Sasha by land. Fang and Serenity were going to keep flying until they got closest to the clearing of the capital of the Firelands. Fang and Serenity spotted dragon guards flying too late, and the two of them searched the ground, seeing Sasha already caught and unable to warn them. Fang was prepared to fight so they could escape and leave Sasha. Serenity put herself in front of Fang to stop him from attempting to kill the guards of the Firelands.

"Fang, no, we go quietly. I'm not going start a war between royals while looking for my brother," said Serenity.

"As you wish, Princess Serenity," said Fang.

The guards were surprised at no resistance but wondered at what the motive was. Based on what they saw, they knew the winged girl was in charge of this group. With no exchange of words, the guards took the intruders to the Firelands to the castle for Lord Dragon II to deal out their punishment. It was only a few minutes' flight over the capital before the guards landed with the three of them in custody in front of the castle. The castle is made up of stone and red ruby; on the outside, the castle has four towers. The two at the front two were shorter than the two in back. The castle had walls on all sides.

CHAPTER SEVENTEEN

WHEN INSIDE THE castle, the three of them got separated. A group of guards took Sasha and Fang to the dungeon and another took Serenity to meet with Lord Dragon II. Serenity knew that if she doesn't behave, this could go south really quickly, but she's not even sure whose lands she was on or who the lord was, so she's not sure if she could keep her temper in check. She's not in the mood to play nice with foreign royals. One of the men guarding her knocked on the chamber's doors.

"Enter," said the voice on the other side.

The guard brought Serenity into the lord's chambers. Serenity took one look and knew that she wasn't going to be able to play nice. Something about his aura frustrated her. She couldn't get a read on him and whether he was a friend or foe.

"Leave us," ordered Lord Dragon II to the guard.

"Vampire girl, what is your name, and why are you in my lands?" demanded Lord Dragon II.

"Why the hell should I tell you?" asked Serenity, frustrated with anger and still not sure what to make of him.

"Do not get mouthy with me, young lady. That attitude won't get you anywhere," snapped Lord Dragon II.

"Go to hell. I don't have to answer to you," snapped Serenity, not thinking before speaking.

"Guard," called Lord Dragon II.

Serenity realized just then she had gone too far and feared she may cost her friends and herself their lives over something so stupid as not showing this lord respect like she was taught at a young age. The guards rushed in.

"Strip-search her," ordered Lord Dragon II.

The guards went for Serenity. Out of impulse or fear, she decided make a run for it without revealing her magic or true form. She busted through the chamber doors and started running to try to find her friends and get them the hell out of this castle and away from Lord Dragon II before they all get the death penalty for trespassing or her for being disrespectful to him. Little did Serenity know that Prince Nightmare III, a man she came to care about, was the son of the lord she totally just disrespected carelessly.

While searching aimlessly, she came across another large hallway, when out of nowhere, a man grabbed her. He was dressed in royal attire. Not recognizing him at first, she started fighting him.

"Calm down, Princess Serenity. You will be safe here, I promise," said Prince Nightmare III sincerely and calmly.

"No, let me go. I need find my friends and leave so none of us get hurt," said Serenity.

"Serenity, look at me. It's me, Nightmare III. I can talk to my father and get him to let your friends go free, but there is someone here I need you to meet," said Prince Nightmare III.

"Fine, but I should probably leave after I was rude and ran my mouth to the lord," said Serenity after looking up at Prince Nightmare III and realizing it was the man she left behind back in Scotland.

Nightmare III led Serenity to the room her brother Scott was staying in while here in the Firelands. Serenity was wondering why he was so insistent on her meeting someone here; she knew no one here in Japan personally. Nightmare III could sense that Serenity was pissed off her friends were imprisoned and confused why he was so insistent of her meeting someone here in the castle.

Only if I knew where my brother is right now, thought Serenity. He's been on her mind since they all had gone their separate ways in America. Nightmare III knocked on the door.

"Come in," said the man on the other side.

When Nightmare III opened the door and they went inside the room, Serenity was surprised to see her brother standing in front of her. It has been fourteen months since she has started her journey to reunite her family after the nightmare in America. She was starting to doubt that she would find him alive and well at all. Serenity started to cry from relief and happiness seeing her younger brother once again. Nightmare

III decided to leave the siblings by showing himself to the door, letting himself out quietly, letting them have time to themselves. He knew he needed to head to his father's chambers and seek an audience with him. Scott was just as surprised to see Serenity once again.

"Sister, please stop crying, we are adults now," asked Scott.

"I know, brother, but I missed you and am so happy to see you alive," said Serenity.

"Yeah, I bet, sister. Have you been staying out of trouble?" asked Scott.

"Hell, no, the VHS have been after me since America. They found me in Scotland and here," said Serenity.

"Oh, sister, and did you get a wolf pet? You got wolf fur on you," asked Scott, pointing out the fact she had gotten wolf fur on her clothing.

"Umm…no, brother, I got a new wolf friend. I've been traveling for a while since I got here," said Serenity.

"Nice, sister. Can we go home in a while? I have to meet someone," asked Scott.

"I guess, but you can't be too long. We still need to travel home. I'm going back to our uncle Jason's castle. I'm not very welcome here after the stunt I pulled in the royal chambers," said Serenity.

"Okay, I understand, sister. You can rest in here for now. I'm going out for a while," said Scott.

"What, brother, let me give you some money for your trip back to our uncle's. It's about a day's walk from here, so you may need to find a place to rest on your way back there," said Serenity.

"Okay, thank you, sister," said Scott before leaving his sister to rest in his guest room.

CHAPTER EIGHTEEN

NIGHTMARE III WAS walking though the hallway glad to see Serenity again but can't help but worry for her safety. He may be able get his father to spare them any harsh penalties for her behavior if he knew the truth to her aggression. He knew that one thing she was trying to keep hidden was her family bloodline and to keep others out of danger from her family's enemies. He knew this only because when he first met Cloud back in Scotland, they fought a hard and long battle; neither of them won over Serenity. Since that day, he's been working with Cloud toward a common goal. So neither has tried killing the other over the past year they had spent together searching for Serenity. When Nightmare III reached his father's chambers, he knocked on the door.

"Come in," answered Lord Dragon II.

Nightmare III entered the room hoping his father won't just dismiss him and let him talk.

"My son, what can I do for you? You know my chambers are off-limits unless it is important," stated Lord Dragon II.

"I know, Father, and this is important. I came here to ask you to let Serenity and her friends off easy. She was only trying to protect the ones around her from her enemies she has, and she was not sure who to trust. She was only scared for the safety of her friends and herself. She is wishing not to reveal more of herself than she must," said Prince Nightmare III.

"Who is this Serenity?" asked Lord Dragon II.

"The vampire girl, and I'm guessing she didn't give you her name and just mouthed off to you then balled out on you," said Princes Nightmare III.

"Yes, that would be her, and why should I let any of them go free?" asked Lord Dragon II, questioning his son's motives.

"Because Serenity and her friends are willing to leave your lands without conflict and return to her uncle's lands. Scott will leave shortly as well since he is the one Serenity came here looking for," said Prince Nightmare III.

"Fine, but Cloud and you must escort Serenity and her friends outside our borders by air. Is that understood? Even if one of them doesn't like heights!" said Lord Dragon II.

"But, Father, that's just cruel and wrong. Why does my girl have to leave anyways right after showing up here?" asked Prince Nightmare III.

"Because she is vampire female, and I hate vampires. End of discussion," said Lord Dragon II.

"Fine, Father," said Prince Nightmare III.

After the long discussion with his father, he left to go find Serenity. Nightmare III started walking back to Scott's room. He wondered if she was still there and if she had gotten any rest yet.

Nightmare III went down the long corridor before reaching Scott's guest room. Because the matter was argent and he needed to get Serenity and her friends out to safety quickly before his father changes his mind on the matter, Nightmare III opened up the door to find that Fang and Sasha have been released from the dungeon. Sasha was cuddling up to Serenity when Nightmare III entered the room, and Fang was standing next to the bed with his wings in, but it was clear he was alert now that he walked in the room. Nightmare III noticed that the wolf didn't bother that Fang was in the room, but his presence did. This bothered Nightmare III the most; he wanted to be the one protecting her and knew that Fang to him will be another rival for her love. The true question was how she felt for them. Nightmare III walked over to Serenity since there was no time to waste to get the four of them out of the Firelands. He gently woke Serenity up, not sure of her reaction to being woken up from sleep.

"What the hell, Nightmare III, I was resting," asked Serenity, sleepy and cranky from being woken up.

"We got to leave. My father doesn't want Fang, Sasha, or you here in the Firelands," said Nightmare III.

"Fine, but Sasha won't be flying—she can't. She also hates heights and hates being carried," said Serenity.

"She doesn't have a choice in the matter. Cloud, Fang, or I have to carry her until we are outside the Firelands," said Nightmare III.

"I trust Fang over Cloud or you carrying her," said Serenity. "Fang, can you please carry Sasha until we get outside the Firelands?" asked Serenity.

"It would be my pleasure," said Fang.

Sasha started whining knowing this meant that she would be in the air.

Nightmare III led the way out of the castle. Nightmare III went to pick up Serenity to carry her, assuming that she can't fly. Serenity slapped his hand, pissed off and able to fly herself. Serenity then ran and took to the sky ready to fly and get fresh air. Following her was Cloud, then Fang carrying Sasha, and finally Nightmare III. Cloud flew close to Serenity but in enough distance so they don't hit wings and go crashing toward the ground. Nightmare III was flying close to Fang carrying Sasha in case Fang needed a hand and to give Serenity some space after pissing her off with waking her up and trying to carry her in flight. After about thirty minutes of flying, they landed three miles outside the Firelands borders. Nightmare III looked at Fang, Cloud, and Sasha, ready to start a fight. Cloud looked to Fang. "Take Serenity and get her somewhere safe. I can handle Nightmare III," said Cloud.

Fang escorted Serenity away from where a fight was about to break out.

CHAPTER NINETEEN

FANG DECIDED TO take Serenity back to her uncle Jason's castle. They walked, and Serenity started to wonder if it was a good idea to leave the others alone back there; she'd seen this scene play out once before. The last time, it almost killed Nightmare III.

"Fang, maybe we should go back. I have a very bad feeling, and even if he is a prince from Japan, he doesn't deserve a fight to death that they are now about to get into," said Serenity.

"Well, we should leave them be. Cloud seems more concerned for your safety over the fact that Nightmare III and him are getting into a death match," said Fang.

"I don't care. They shouldn't kill each other over something stupid as me or not knowing how I truly feel about each of you," said Serenity.

"Do you think it will change anything going back there now?" asked Fang.

"It may not change the fact that they are fighting, but I would at least like to make sure no one dies," said Serenity.

"I think for your safety, it's better to stay at your uncle Jason's castle after what went down in the Firelands," said Fang.

"Fine, you are probably right," said Serenity.

Fang and Serenity made it to the castle before Lord Hathaway's guards stopped them. Once they recognized that it was Princess Serenity, they let her pass but arrested Fang out of the blue. It didn't help that he didn't come with her the first time, and they were prepared to take Fang before the lord for judgment.

Fang was worried that this could cause trouble for him; the Capulet family and his family were sworn enemies. He wasn't sure what this was going to mean for the Hathaway family. Sometimes different lands mean nothing, and he could still be treated as an enemy here. Since the fact that Lord Hathaway hasn't gone after wolf, he was pretty sure he'd be safe if he played his cards right. This meant it would be best to not reveal his true feelings for the princess.

CHAPTER TWENTY

CLOUD, SASHA, AND Nightmare III all took battle stances facing each other and bowed to one another. Cloud then took to the sky. Nightmare III decided to go for Sasha first since she was a female and looked like an easy target. Cloud was only interested in fighting Nightmare III, but he couldn't fight the way he likes with Sasha nearby, afraid he would harm her in the process. Nightmare III pulled out his long sword hoping it would be enough to take down Sasha. Sasha automatically pulled out her guns to fight with first, but she knew her skills were only good for long-distance attacks. Best she could do was dodge Nightmare III's attack and counterattack with bullets. Cloud was using his magic on Nightmare III to try to wear down Nightmare III, hating using Sasha as a decoy at the moment; but with her around, and if he got into a sword fight, everyone in range could be in danger of being cut by the sword he owned. After a while, Sasha ran out of bullets and started offloading her throwing stars and daggers on Nightmare III; even with Cloud using his magic on Nightmare III, Sasha's attacks ended up being no more than surface wounds. As a last resort, Sasha brought out a sword to try and fight back. Nightmare III grabbed it by the blade, annoyed with her efforts and assuming the blade wouldn't be able to cut him. He was proven wrong, but it wasn't one that could cut him deeply without repeatedly hitting him.

Cloud descended to the ground, and without adding magic to his sword, he got in the middle of the fight between Sasha and Nightmare III, knowing she won't last long. He grabbed the handle of Sasha's sword.

"Sasha, go now and leave the rest to me. Make sure you don't take a direct route back to Lord Hathaway's lands," ordered Cloud.

Sasha did as she was ordered, sensing it was unwise to argue the point with Cloud. She also had the feeling if she stayed, she would be getting in the way and putting herself in danger. The one thing wolves knew best was to follow their instincts.

When Sasha was far enough away, Cloud and Nightmare III started going at it. Cloud was no longer holding back, sensing the only one that will be getting hurt now was his target. Cloud knew he had the upper hand and started toying with Nightmare III to make him regret picking a fight with him, so if even by some miracle he survived, he would think twice before starting another fight with him. He wished that Nightmare III learned from their first battle back in Scotland and never picked this fight. He knew this may end up hurting Serenity once she finds out the truth. Cloud started by landing a deep cut in Nightmare's left arm. To Nightmare III's surprise, it was not healing on its own and was gushing out blood. Cloud landed one on the right arm, then left leg, then right leg. As the fight continued, Nightmare III's body became heavy, too much for him to keep standing with the loss of blood. As Nightmare III fell toward Cloud, heading face-first toward the ground, Cloud landed one swift attack to the chest, going for the heart. Cloud's blade went through, but Nightmare III landed unconscious on Cloud. Cloud pushed him off and toward the ground, going on his back this time. Cloud made sure he had his sword out of Nightmare III before pushing him to the ground. Cloud then collected all the weapons that were used during the long battle and took off to a nearby stream to clean them. He made sure it was far enough away that no help that came would find him. But he didn't plan to linger longer than it would take to clean the weapons, then he headed back to Lord Hathaway's lands.

CHAPTER TWENTY-ONE

BACK IN THE Firelands, everyone was getting ready to go to bed but Exotic, who talked Scott into going out. When Exotic was sure her parents have gone to bed for the night, she went to Scott's guest room to get him. They were going to sneak out a secret passage way she knew of. Scott quietly shut his bedroom door so as not to alert the guards at the end of hall. It took them ten minutes of walking the hallways and avoiding the guards before reaching the secret passageway door. Exotic opened the door, and Scott went in first. After she got in, she made sure the door was shut behind her. After making a few wrong turns and ten minutes later, they exited the secret passageway. The lighting in the passageway was very dim, so it was easy to get lost if one was not paying attention.

They were now free to hang out in the village for a while before returning to the castle to get some rest. Scott wondered what was going to happen when he had to leave the castle.

Exotic led Scott around the village, just hanging out. When they came across a group of kids, Exotic and Scott started playing with them. Since they were away from the castle, it gave them the freedom to do things like normal people do and not be defined by the rules of the castle. The way Scott and Exotic were together, they could be a perfect match, but everyone, including themselves, was oblivious on how good they were for each other.

CHAPTER TWENTY-TWO

SERENITY WAS IN her guest room at her uncle Jason's castle. Serenity went on her laptop. She booked five guest rooms. The first room she booked was her private room, then when someone suddenly knocked on the door to her room, Serenity got up and answered the door. She was a little disappointed to see it was one of the massagers of the royal family.

"Princess Serenity, Lord Hathaway wishes for you to attend the royal ball that's being held tonight," said the massager.

"As he wishes. I'll get ready at once," said Princess Serenity.

The massager left Princess Serenity with nothing else needing to be said. Serenity knew she couldn't refuse her uncle's wishes; he was a lord—and not only that, he had given her sanctuary while in Japan even though the VHS were hunting down her and her family. The only thing she never told her uncle was it was her father's, Jonathan's, fault for feeding on people outside even if it was in dark alleyways. He never had restraint to take them into a private room to feed. She hated her father. But she couldn't remember anything before the age of four. The only thing she really remembered was a lullaby her mother sang to her. But even spending time with her mother stopped after the age of four.

Since then, she dealt with being alone with Scott growing up or hiding in her big brother Jonathan's room. Johnathan's room was her sanctuary. When it came down to it, since she was four, she always got in trouble for one reason or another. Serenity always found one way or another to sneak into the village; she loved being among the people. But for one reason or another, her father disapproved of the fact of her being outside the castle without guards or just in general. It was like he was trying to hide her from something.

She didn't bring any of her royal dresses, but that never mattered when the occasion called for it. Serenity just pictures the outfit she wanted to wear, and it would appear in the room on her bed, and any shoe she liked would be on the floor right under the dress she wanted to wear. For tonight, she picked one that was not pronounced that she was a princess. Serenity chose a dress that didn't have sleeves but attached by a jeweled neckband that was in the shape of a V in front and round in the back. The dress itself was violet; there were silver jewels in the pattern of the flower sequins throughout the dress. Serenity put up her hair with braids coming down from both sides and left the rest of her hair loose. She knew there was only so much she could do to hide her identity. Serenity walked the hallways of the castle that she was not completely familiar with. Serenity knew she couldn't blow it tonight; she was not sure what her uncle was getting out of this, or if it was a distraction, but when it came down to it, her options were limited.

Serenity walked in the ball seeing a few dozen people from all country of origins. They were royals from many countries here. As far as Serenity could tell, this was planned way before she arrived in his lands for the first time a week ago. She had also been in Japan the last few months, and if her family received any invitation, no one had been home for any length of time over the last year. Her parents had still not returned, and without lord and lady, the lands may fall into chaos. When Serenity walked in, everyone's eyes turned to her. She never attended a ball back in Russia; she was forbidden by her father, Jonathan, but never understood why.

A lord that was in attendance was from her country. He walked toward her wanting to speak with her. Serenity was not sure whether to talk to the lord or ignore him, but here, of all places, she couldn't be rude. Lord Hathaway got between her and the lord from Russia. She sensed Lord Hathaway didn't want something revealed to her. What she did next would surprise everyone later if they realized it or even could recall the night. She used magic to freeze time on everyone in the room but the lord that was trying to approach her when Lord Hathaway tried to interrupt. She walked out to the garden not caring if the lord took her invitation at a chance to talk with no interruptions.

CHAPTER TWENTY-THREE

SASHA AND CLOUD met up again at the halfway point to Lord Hathaway's lands, coming from different directions to evade capture and ensure at least one made it back to help Serenity with her journey. Sasha was surprised to see Cloud again so soon; it had only been a few hours since they split up outside the Firelands after the brutal battle with Nightmare III.

"Cloud, how did you find me again so soon?" asked Sasha.

"A falcon like me who's highly skilled can track someone from far away. I actually tracked you ever since we split up, so I didn't accidentally run into you on way back to main path to Lord Hathaway lands too soon in case one of us was followed," said Cloud.

"I didn't realize you were a bird," said Sasha with a giggle.

"Sasha, here are your weapons. I cleaned them for you," said Cloud.

"Cloud, you didn't have to do this. I considered them lost when I left the battlefield," said Sasha.

"I know, but I wanted to, and it was wiser to take all the weapons then leave Lord Dragon II with some way to figure out who attacked his son," said Cloud.

Sasha took her weapons from Cloud realizing he really thought out every possible outcome in the midst of a battle and took the best possible action to ensure as much as possible this didn't blow back on him and her. Sasha put all her weapons back in place from where she had them before the fight. Sasha and Cloud started finishing the last march back to Lord Hathaway's lands. It was pushing dawn as they reached the entrance to the Hathaway lands. They made it back to the Hathaway lands with ease. Now came the hard part—making it close to the Hathaway castle and the village that surrounded it before being captured by the Firelands guards. That is, if they haven't even started searching for the group that Nightmare III escorted out of the castle. Cloud and Sasha made it back into the village where the Hathaway castle was within a thirty-minute walk from the border entrance. Cloud looked at Sasha, and they both stopped.

"Sasha, please, let me take you out to breakfast before we go to the castle and meet up with Serenity," asked Cloud.

"Okay, sounds like a good plan to me," said Sasha.

Cloud showed Sasha the way to his favorite café. Sasha and Cloud were becoming friends quickly, not having known each other for very long. When they entered the café, Cloud got a table for two with a view of the village. He wanted see the rush of the morning market in the village. When the waiter came over, he ordered two coffees. He also placed his breakfast order—a specialty breakfast sandwich that contained every meat they served: bacon, sausage, ham, turkey, salami, and baloney with American cheese. A side order of hash browns, bagel with cream cheese, and sausage links. They started talking like old friends while Sasha looked over the menu and was waiting for coffee to arrive. The waiter came back a few minutes later, and Sasha ordered a high-protein and carb breakfast.

After they got their breakfast and ate it all, they came to an agreement that they both would stay with her until she brings her family fully back together in Russia, then they decided where to go from there. Cloud's family knew a deep dark past about Serenity's family and the truth about her relation to Jonathan, but his folks made him swear not tell her the truth; she needed to keep her true identity a secret until the time was right and she'd finally find her own way back to the Land of Crystal and Ice in Russia. Once they were finished eating, Cloud paid, and they walked back to the Hathaway castle together.

Back in Lord Hathaway's chambers before the ball, Fang was face-to-face with Lord Hathaway to find out what will happen to him knowing he came way too close to the castle; only if he thought it through, he would have Serenity return from the village alone. He didn't know how he was going get out of this if Lord Hathaway was anything like Lord Capulet. He always avoided Lord Capulet's guards and castle. Lord Hathaway looked Fang over and could easily tell he was one of his brother-in-law's enemies, but he was wondering why this man protected his niece from danger in a foreign land instead of killing her. Lord Hathaway was wondering if this man somehow had feelings for the enemy's daughter. That wouldn't be an enemy. If she knew the truth, their families could potentially ally against his brother, even though this fact should concern Lord Hathaway, but it didn't. If anything, at the moment, he indebted to this man for keeping his niece safe. Lord Hathaway looked at Fang with aberration.

"Fang, since you show loyalty to my niece and is an ally to her, I'll give you the option either to leave my land and not return to my castle or you can be handed over to my guards and stay in my dungeon until my brother-in-law can be reached," said Lord Hathaway.

"I'll leave your lands and never return to your castle again," said Fang.

"You are free to leave and will be escorted out of the castle and the lands by my guards," said Lord Hathaway.

"As you wish, Lord Hathaway," said Fang.

"Guards," ordered Lord Hathaway.

A few of the royal guard entered the chambers swiftly and quickly.

"Yes, my lord," said the guards.

"You shall escort this man out of my lands, but you are not allowed under any circumstance to kill him, he is not a danger to my lands or its citizens," said Lord Hathaway.

"As you wish, my lord," said the guard.

"Please follow us," asked the guard facing Fang.

There was no need for further conversation, so Fang followed the guards back to the palace entrance. The guards and he left the palace and started heading for the land's borders. Fang knew this was the best possible outcome given his position and circumstance behind it. The lands he was allowed to enter, thank God, was far away from the Firelands; he was wondering what was the outcome of the battle with Prince Nightmare III and Cloud. Fang headed for the hotel he's been staying before he met up with Serenity. He only planned to stay there until she left her uncle Jason's lands.

CHAPTER TWENTY-FOUR

LORD DRAGON II sent out a search party to look for his son and find out why he's been unable to return home. He knew his son should been home by now. Lord Dragon II was worried that his son may be injured or dead at this point. Lord Dragon II spared no effort to bring his son home; he sent hundreds of his men out to search for his son, who can be an idiot at times and gets himself into trouble. He sent thirty groups of twenty soldiers after his son. Each group consisted of six healers, three of them are dragons and three are falcons, and six highly trained trackers. Seven groups were sent in four directions—north, east, west, and south. The remaining two were sent to the east and west as support teams. Knowing his lands bordered four other lords, he sent his soldiers out in civilian clothes, having them conceal their weapons. After an hour of searching, a group to the east found the prince lying in a pool of his own blood.

The twelve healers started working on all of Prince Nightmare III's injuries. The twelve trackers fanned out trying to find any trace of the one or ones that did this to their prince. What they were able find out was that it was the handiwork of a magic user. They couldn't pick up any trace of the group that Prince Nightmare III escorted outside the lands. The guards started to wonder if they played a role in it. Instead of following the magic trail, they returned to the rest of the group. They needed see to Prince Nightmare III and return him home safely before chasing after the group that attacked him. They hoped the lord will have a clue what to do about the group Prince Nightmare III associated with.

It had taken the healers three hours to heal all injuries, including repairing the prince's heart. No weapons should have been able to pierce the prince's skin. After all the repairs were done, Prince Nightmare III was still out cold. It took four of the guards to carry the prince back to the castle. It took two more hours to travel home with the prince since he was out cold and had to be carried. He looked as if he only would weigh about 250 lbs. of pure muscle, but appearances can be deceiving. The leader of the two groups that found him was going have to report their findings to Lord Dragon II, and they didn't want to be around his wrath when he'd be pissed off. The healers weren't even sure if the prince would wake. The four carrying the prince broke away from the group once they reached the castle. They took the prince to his private chambers in the hopes it would help him come around with warmth and safety of someplace familiar to him.

The leaders reached Lord Dragon II's chambers after separating from their groups to give a report to Lord Dragon II. The one that was a higher-rank officer knocked on the door.

"Come in," said Lord Dragon II from the other side of the door.

The guards entered the lord's chambers, hesitant on giving the report on Prince Nightmare II's condition.

"Report your findings to me," ordered Lord Dragon II.

"We found Prince Nightmare III lying in a pool of his own blood, like he was being toyed with by a trained guard or knight that has no mercy for a life of another. We also found no trace of culprit or culprits. Furthermore, the group your son escorted out of the lands can't be located," said the guard.

"By royal decree, do not let Cloud return to these lands until we can find out who nearly killed my son before the healers reversed all the physical damage done to him," ordered Lord Dragon II.

"Yes, sir," said the leader of the guards before leaving the lord's chambers to give the direct order to the rest of the royal guard and soldiers.

The head of the royal guard hoped the one the prince cared for wasn't in the middle of this mess. But he couldn't help but have the feeling one of her companions had something to do with this, or at least two of them; even if the second one didn't land any blows, it may just have been used as a decoy.

CHAPTER TWENTY-FIVE

BACK IN THE Hathaway lands, time stood still because Serenity froze it, sick of people hiding stuff from her and willing to take the risk meeting a Russian lord alone in the Hathaway Garden. She knew if anyone new entered the Hathaway land without her sensing them, they won't be affected by her magic. Much to her surprise, the Russian lord took her bait to talk alone.

"We only got twenty minutes, then the spell I casted will release, and time will resume, and if we aren't where we were standing by then, Lord Hathaway will recognize a time spell was cast," said Serenity.

"That's fine. I just want you to answer me a few questions, then we will return to the ballroom," said the lord.

"Okay, I'll answer your questions to the best of my ability," said Serenity.

"Why do you stay as Lord Johnathan Capulet's daughter? Don't you know anything about your past?" asked Lord Vasiliev.

"What would you know of my family? I certainly don't know what you are talking about," said Serenity.

"The Belikov princess doesn't even know the truth herself. I guess it can't be helped. I guess I'll have to drop it for now, but if you are back in Russia and ever need assistance, come to the land of silver and stars, but make sure to be in your true form when you enter, or it will be painful the way the land will make you reveal yourself," said the lord.

"Will you give me your name, my lord?" asked Princess Serenity.

"Sorry, princess, but for now, while you're in the lands of the Hathaways, my family and I must insist to remain a stranger," said Lord Vasiliev.

"As you wish. Let's return to the ballroom before we run out of time and I put you in danger with my uncle," said Princess Serenity.

"As you wish, princess," said Lord Vasiliev.

They both walked back into the ballroom and got back into their place, then the magic was lifted, with Lord Hathaway between them again furious as ever.

"Lord Vasiliev, you weren't invited here to my ball. Why bring your presence here?" demanded Lord Hathaway.

"That's a need-to-know. If it's really that much of an inconvenience for you, I'll take my leave of your lands and return to my cousin's lands here in Japan. I came with his family to your ball," said Lord Vasiliev.

"Just leave. I don't want any Russian lords present at my ball tonight," ordered Lord Hathaway.

It was now clear that he was trying to keep Serenity from learning the truth of her past. Even so, Lord Vasiliev knew his attempt wasn't futile. Just the small talk to her was clear that she possessed the ability to see versions of the past, present, and future. He just prayed that she can survive that family long enough to find the truth she seeks.

Serenity mingled with the guests at the ball but felt so out of place, so she walked out to the garden to get some fresh air and some space. She started feel as if the family she knew as hers was a lie. She hoped her brother comes to meet her soon; she was ready to return home to resupply and go after Janine and Jonathan; Scott's parents. She didn't know she was heading for a trap going into the garden. A man appeared in front of her. He had long golden hair with silver highlights, pale skin, black wings, eyes with the color of a shining star. He had a blue-gold-blue top with silver rings, then a gold ring then a gold star in the middle; in between each ring was silver. He wore blue bottoms.

She knew there were guards nearby, but they didn't pick up on his presence. This didn't alarm her right off. She was able to see spirits of the dead since she was a child. The man turned the garden into the oracle temple. She was unsure why she was back in the temple that she escaped from a few days ago when she refused to join them. She never expected them to come after her or how it was possible do so in a royal garden, not near a temple.

"Is the oracle princess surprised to see one of us here?" asked the male oracle.

"How can you guys reach me here?" demanded Serenity.

"So you can't see what's going to happen in the present if it involves you," said the male oracle.

"What do you know of my abilities?" demanded Serenity.

"Well, well, the princess has a tongue on her. This will still do nicely, though you can't change what is to come or to be," said the male oracle.

Serenity's senses became heightened and alert face-to-face with this oracle. The spirit of a Russian male appeared before her and the male oracle. She recognized him from the temple.

"Father," said Serenity in a whisper.

"My daughter, I can't break this secret space nor can I fight an oracle at this time," said the spirit.

"Spirit, leave the girl to her fate. It is sealed," said the male oracle.

"I know my daughter's fate is sealed, but I beg of you to let her leave the temple after," said the spirit.

"Is that all you are asking of me, Lord Belikov?" said the male oracle.

"Yes, since I know what is coming, I can't stop being my physical body is encased in ice, and crystal is restricting me," said the spirit.

"As you wish, your daughter will be allowed to return to the world of the living, but she will be going through changes. You do understand what she is receiving from us," asked the male oracle.

"I am well aware of her duties as a descendant of oracles who has received their abilities," said the spirit.

The oracle kept the conviction he had with the spirit from reaching her ears, knowing what her father had to ask of him didn't concern her. The spirit went over to Serenity wanting to say something to her in private before leaving his daughter once more.

"My daughter, be strong. I am sorry that I couldn't change your fate. This fate is due to your bloodline. Please don't curse who you are after learning the truth of your bloodline. My dear child," said the spirit before disappearing.

Serenity couldn't wrap her head around what the spirit said to her, but she wouldn't have time to figure out before what came next. The oracle advanced on her. She looked around see if she could leave the temple. But where it was, was a secret place for oracles, and she didn't create the entrance herself; she realized she couldn't escape.

"Princess, relax, this would be easier on you if you just let me," said the male oracle.

"I can't accept this, specially not knowing you," said Serenity.

"Since the time I put up this barrier, no none can enter or leave the Hathaway lands. The Hathaway ball will last as long as we need," said the male oracle.

"If this is so, then can I know your name and know why it has to be us?" asked Serenity.

"Are you resigning to your fate?" asked the male oracle.

"No, not just yet. I want to learn the truth before I go through with it," said Serenity, just then realizing she was starting to accept her fate.

"My name is Prince Yasha Vasiliev II, and because shortly after a certain man was frozen in time by his enemy, he came to me and my father begging us to keep his oracle line pure and among allies," said Prince Yasha II.

"How is an oracle line broken?" asked Serenity.

"If the first oracle child isn't from same origins as their mate also being pure Russian," said Prince Yasha II.

"What happens if I don't willingly cooperate?" asked Serenity.

"How much control do you have on your own magic?" asked Prince Yasha II.

"Depends. Sometimes I lose control of it if scared, upset, or frightened," said Serenity.

Please, Lord Belikov, help me get through to your daughter, thought Prince Yasha, not wanting this to put her or him in danger.

"Please, Serenity, just let me help you before another oracle with worse intentions for you try to intervene," pleaded Prince Yasha II.

Prince Yasha's wish was answered, but he wouldn't know it. Just to Serenity alone, her father appeared once more. The prince couldn't see him this time and won't be able to hear him.

"My poor daughter, please heed his words, they all are true. If it isn't him here and now after he leaves the land has been marked by the temple you be in further danger as unmated oracle child. You are of prime age to receive the oracle blessing of a child. It may not be the path you wish to walk without love, but it's not a path we can choose as descendants of the oracle line, but it is one you are destined to walk," said her father's spirit.

"Is he the one you would wish of me to mate, Father?" asked Serenity.

"Yes, for your safety, I wish it to be the prince you don't know," said her father's spirit.

"Then I'll try to cooperate with him," said Serenity.

"It's okay to feel the way you do now. Your mother felt the same way," said her father before disappearing once more, leaving her feeling alone.

"Prince Yasha II, take it slow with me, and I'll try my best to accept you, but I'm not promising I won't have a reaction to this," said Serenity in a shaky voice.

"I promise I'll take it slow, and no other will be allowed to enter the temple from this sight as long as I'm nearby," said Prince Yasha II.

CHAPTER TWENTY-SIX

YASHA WAS BEING as gentle with Serenity as possible. At this moment, he was fighting every instinct of an archangel oracle male that was ready to mate with a female of his choice for the first time. He started by gently kissing Serenity to give her a distraction from everything he was going to have do to her in order to prepare her for mating. He had never mated before, but every instinct in his body was telling him exactly what to do. He wanted to take it slow, but every urge was telling him to take her here and now.

Yasha II started by using magic to remove her clothes without destroying them. He knew she would need them to rejoin the ball when done. He ran his hands down her body, running over every curve and inch of her, working his way over her breast down her sides and over her stomach, making his way to her core. He gently spread her legs and slid two of his fingers in her core and moving them in and out. Starting out slow with his fingers and increasing speed, he used his hands little by little until she was primed and begging for it. In order to make it worse on it, he was sending gentle waves of magic, matching his motions with his fingers.

After about a half hour of just using his hand to pleasure her and make her beg for more, he removed his hand and thrust his junk into her core. With no warning to her, he turned form gentleman to pure urge taking control. He lost what self-control he had; it disappeared after penetrating her. He couldn't help but go at her until she was sore and can no longer move. They both were sweaty and panting after he finished with her. Yasha II didn't want to leave her now that he has mated her, but he knew it was safer to watch over her from a safe distance than to be part of her life at this time. He also knew that even though it was not right to do, he must alter the memories of someone close to her recently to temporarily take his place when he's not available.

He looked into her memories to see who she'd been in contact with recently. He saw through her memories that only two males could qualify as a fill-in. He chose to have Fang to be a replacement while he was away. He couldn't alter Serenity's memories of tonight's events, but he was sure he could convince her to use Fang as substitute. Serenity looked at him shocked by what happened and was not sure how to respond to just doing it with this man that was basically a complete stranger. She went flush thinking about what just occurred between them.

"Serenity, we need to keep the fact that you have mated with an oracle secret, do you understand?" asked Yasha II.

"Why is it that I feel like I don't want you to leave me?" asked Serenity.

"That feeling won't go away anytime soon. But for your safety, I have to keep my distance until the right time. I'll be watching over you still, just not where anybody can see me," said Yasha II.

Serenity was not sure what was going on with her, but she knew her friends will have to help her. She was hoping the whole fate details weren't true. She didn't need to be made a mother just yet and carrying a stranger's child or children. She felt like the whole world she knew was turned upside down.

"Yasha II, can I return to the garden at my uncle's castle now?" asked Serenity.

"If that is what you wish, I'll release you from the temple," said Yasha II.

"Yes, that is what I wish," said Serenity.

Serenity walked inside and decided she needed to leave the Hathaway castle right away and possibly even the lands. She didn't report to her uncle what happened, she just returned to her guest room right away. Serenity walked from the ballroom to her guest room unescorted. She lay down on her bed once she got there, knowing some rest would do her justice.

Serenity woke up a little before sunrise, wanting to explore the lands more while waiting for her brother to meet her and hoping Cloud and Sasha would return soon; she would like to return to Russia. She wanted to go after Jonathan and Janine soon; she needed to know the truth, and they would have the answers. Serenity felt so out of place around the vampires, but there was nothing she could do to change that fact. She found using vampire form taxing; she didn't like drinking blood, and her power didn't come from vampires.

Serenity was realizing her roots weren't of a vampire like Jonathan and Janine. She wanted to know the exact origins of her bloodline. Serenity sneaked out of the castle since most everyone was asleep. She hoped she didn't find trouble being alone, but it never was the way that goes for her; she could find trouble even with her companions around. She thought back to when Nightmare III started a fight with Cloud, Sasha, and Fang. Cloud was acting as protector when he ordered Fang to get her back to the Hathaway lands safely. She wished that she was able find out if Nightmare III was alive, but that would be hard when they think she is a vampire.

Serenity ended up wandering into another temple in the Hathaway lands; this time she was alone and not sure what was drawing her in. No one was there to stop her or protect her. Behind her she heard a sound like the path she came from just was blocked off by a trap she hit or a spirit set the trap off intently; now the only way she could go was forward. She was as carious as a cat, and that had always gotten her into trouble.

CHAPTER TWENTY-SEVEN

SASHA AND CLOUD made it to the Hathaway castle and into the main hallway to talk to a maid to seek info on Fang and Serenity. A maid stopped them before they could go any farther in to find out their business, with the master having royal guests here for the next three-day events of balls.

"Cloud, who are you looking for?" inquired the maid.

"We are here to see Princess Serenity and Fang," said Cloud.

"You missed Princess Serenity. I'm pretty sure she left the castle before dawn, and as far as Fang goes, he is banished from these lands—if he wishes to stay alive and out of Lord Jonathan's grip," said the maid.

"Do you know where she would have gone?" asked Cloud.

"No, not really. My lord may be able to give you a better starting point than I can," said the maid.

"Okay, thanks for your help," said Cloud.

Cloud and Sasha just stood there looking at each other trying to think of their next move.

"Sasha, I'll go speak to Lord Hathaway, see where Serenity would most likely go. Please wait here. I'll be back soon," said Cloud.

"Okay, sounds good since Lord Hathaway hates me for being a wolf that has a human form and can talk," said Sasha.

"I'll do almost anything for a cute little wolf girl," said Cloud.

He then walked off toward Lord Hathaway's chambers, knowing right where it was. Cloud has been here a dozen times before. He reached the chambers within a few minutes. Once he stopped in front of the door, he knocked on it.

"Yes, come in," said Lord Hathaway.

Cloud walked into Lord Hathaway's chambers to seek an audience with him. Lord Hathaway was not one bit surprised that it was Cloud this early in the morning. But he was not sure why Cloud has come to him.

"Cloud, what can I do for you this early in the morning?" asked Lord Hathaway.

"Would you know where your niece has gone here in your lands? One of the maids said she wasn't in her guest room," asked Cloud.

"If I had to guess, I would say exploring the old ruins here. I have asked her not to go near them. Knowing her, she doesn't heed warnings to stay away from them," said Lord Hathaway, concerned for her safety.

"Okay, thank you, Lord Hathaway. I'll find her and make sure she is safe," said Cloud.

"Thank you, Cloud," said Lord Hathaway, relieved that someone was looking out for his niece.

Cloud rushed out of the chambers to meet up with Sasha to go after Serenity. He was able to get a lead on her location from her uncle Jason.

"So, do you know where they are?" asked Sasha.

"I found out Fang left the lands so he can still help Serenity once she leaves to head home. But Serenity may be in danger. Lord Hathaway thinks she may have gone off and explored the ruins alone. We don't have any time to waste. If there are any malicious spirits down in the ruins, Serenity's bound to be in trouble," said Cloud.

"Then let's not waste time and go after her," said Sasha.

Cloud and Sasha left in a hurry hoping to get to Serenity before something bad happened to her. Cloud led the way since he knew where the ruins were in the Hathaway lands. Once they reached the ruins, Cloud noticed that if anyone went inside, the footprints had been blown away by now. He wondered how long ago she entered the ruins. To him, the ruins looked sealed off. This meant that the spirits inside were up to no good and Serenity was their target. He was hoping if he and Sasha get close to the ruins, it would let them in as well. Cloud grabbed Sasha's hand due to wanting to get into the ruins and not to be separated right off. He also added a tracking spell to her wrist; that way if they got separated in the ruins, he could find her.

When they got close to the ruins, the doors that looked sealed tight to Cloud opened. Cloud knew this could be a trap. Out of nowhere, a mysterious man appeared before Sasha and Cloud. They were startled by a stranger who had long golden hair and silver highlights, pale skin, black wings, eyes the color of a shining star, a blue-gold-blue top with a silver ring, then a gold ring then a gold star in the middle; in between each ring was is silver. He wore blue bottoms.

"Cool it, Cloud, I am not your enemy," said Prince Yasha II.

"Who are you anyways, and how do you know my name?" demanded Cloud.

"Well, that's a decision for Serenity after she is out of the ruins. If she's not in danger by spirits, she will be by the oracles," said Prince Yasha II.

"What the hell are you talking about?" said Cloud.

"I'll explain everything after Serenity is safe. I have my own reasons ensuring her safety," said Prince Yasha II.

"Fine, we will finish this after she is safely out of the ruins," said Cloud.

Yasha II marked both Sasha and Cloud without them knowing it to ensure their safety in the ruins from the oracles that could choose to harm them or make it so they couldn't leave the ruins. Spirits aren't only treated when it comes to exploring ancient ruins you had be warry of oracles that inhabit the temples in ruins. The three of them entered the ruins cautiously. Prince Yasha II hoped all they'd encounter would be spirits; it's better than coming across other oracles.

CHAPTER TWENTY-EIGHT

SERENITY WAS DEEP in the ruins when all of a sudden a noise came from under her. She was not sure what the noise was, but she knew it was not good; she also knew that she couldn't return the way she came. Serenity took off in a run to try to either find a way out or find what made the noise under her. After a few minutes, she realized she was in trouble. A spirit appeared in front of her. He was a boy looking like he could be evil and pull her under and kill her without anyone knowing until after it has been too late. Serenity sensed that others also have entered the ruins. She knew she needed to stop this spirit to save the others who entered the ruins after she did. She didn't know that the ones that have entered were Yasha II, Cloud, and Sasha. She knew she needed to figure out what the spirit wanted to save everyone. The spirit didn't go to hurt Serenity but disappeared, intending on leading her somewhere farther away from her friends.

Serenity ran farther into the ruins and suddenly realized she'd been here before. But now she was feeling trapped; she knew she couldn't use some of her special abilities this far in the ruins. The spirit was the key to leaving the ruins safely and saving the others that came in possibly after her. The spirit came up to her laughing, knowing he got her to himself.

"Boy, what are you here for, and why did you lead me so deep into the ruins?" asked Serenity.

***

Nightmare III woke up, surprised to be alive, knowing Cloud did come close to killing him and beat him badly in a fight, toying with him, not showing him any mercy after he was the one that instigated the fight. He couldn't believe that his father's men were able to revive him. He knew this meant he may die again at the hands of another if he decided to go after Serenity. Damn, he wanted be with her but knew her protector was too strong for him to take on, even if it was a fair one-on-one fight. He wondered if it was even worth going after Serenity after he regains his strength.

His father walked in his room and was pissed about the mess he got into over a female vampire.

"My son, what were you thinking getting involved with that vampire girl?" asked Nightmare II.

"I love her and thought she could love me back, but no one wants me to get close to her," said Nightmare II.

"Sorry, son, but next time, we may not be able to save you. Do you still wish to chase after her and risk your life for her?" asked Nightmare II.

"Yes, Father, I do, because I want her as mine, and no one else is to be able to have her," said Nightmare II.

"Okay, please be careful out there," said Nightmare II.

"I will, Father, I promise," said Nightmare III.

Lord Dragon II was still worried about his son's fate. This girl could very well be the death of his son.

CHAPTER TWENTY-NINE

IT'S AROUND 1:00 a.m. when Scott and Exotic sneaked back into the castle after spending the last few hours outside playing with orphans and even some runaway children. Exotic and Scott stopped outside of Scott's guest room. Scott invited Exotic to join him for the night. He was leaning against the door holding it open. Exotic stood there thinking for a moment if she should. Scott wondered if she would take him up on his offer. Without saying a word to him, she walked past him and entered the room. Scott stepped in and quickly shut the door, knowing he will have to soon leave the Firelands and reunite with his sister to return home.

Exotic walked over to the bed. She took off her shoes then lay down, exhausted from the long day they had. Scott removed his shoes, socks, pants, jacket, and T-shirt then lay with her. Scott was hating the idea of having to leave Exotic behind, but he was not sure if his sister had enough to bring another passage home with them. He didn't even know if she had any travel companions that will be returning to Russia with them. Scott was gentle holding Exotic. Exotic fell asleep right away in his arms, feeling safe with him holding her. She would soon find out he had to leave the Firelands and return home to Russia with his sister.

***

Cloud, Sasha, and Yasha II found an area that was blocked off, and they couldn't go any farther. Cloud started cursing knowing a spirit was blocking them from going any farther.

"Cloud, are you able to sense the magic here as well?" asked Yasha II.

"Yes, but I can't tell if Serenity is beyond it or if she's safe. I'm pretty sure at this point she may be alone with a spirit," said Cloud.

"I hope that's all that finds her down there," said Yasha II, worried if she goes too far, oracles will approach her.

"Wait, are you saying there can be other things down there too?" asked Cloud.

"Yes, but if it's just spirits, then she will be okay," said Yasha II.

"Please tell us what else she could be facing down there," said Cloud.

"That is a need-to-know basis, and it is not for you to know," said Yasha II.

"Fine, can you at least find out that she's okay?" said Cloud.

"Maybe. If my preestablished connection with her is not being blocked," said Yasha II.

"What have you done to her?" demanded Cloud, being her protector.

"Cloud, calm down," said Sasha.

"No, not until he tells me what's going on," said Cloud.

"I won't go into detail, Cloud, but all you need to know is she needs to be protected, and the rest will come out in time," said Yasha II.

Not caring of consequences or thinking before acting, Cloud punched Yasha square in the nose. Yasha threw Cloud back twenty feet.

"Cool it, Cloud. What happened between her and I was for her safety as well as for fulfilling a promise to her father," said Yasha II.

"Jonathan's the last person I would do anything for! Why did you?" demanded Cloud.

"Cloud, do you even know the truth of Serenity's bloodline?" asked Yasha II.

"No, why, Yasha II?" asked Cloud.

"What I did wasn't a promise to Lord Capulet but to Lord Belikov," said Yasha II.

"Are you even suggesting Serenity is Lord Belikov's daughter? He's been encased in crystal and ice for the last thirty years," said Cloud.

"Yes, and it is true," said Yasha II.

"I'm not going to argue with you over the truth because it will reveal itself in time. But do what you can for Serenity," said Cloud.

Yasha II was glad Cloud was leaving it to him, but he could only do so much if she was not in the temple.

CHAPTER THIRTY

SERENITY FOUND HERSELF face-to-face with the spirit of a young boy. She approached the spirit cautiously. She was hoping if she communicated with the spirit, it would save her and the ones that came in after her.

"Little boy, what's keeping you attached to this world? Let me help you move on," said Serenity.

"How can you help me?" asked the boy meanly.

"I have special abilities that I could help you," said Serenity.

"I have been waiting here for someone to return," said the boy.

"Who are you waiting for and why?" asked Serenity.

"A Russian friend of mine that promised she would be back to see me, but before that could happen, I was murdered. Her name was Serenity Irshrose Capulet," said the boy.

"That is my name, and how long have you been dead?" asked Serenity.

"I couldn't tell you how many years it's been," said the boy.

"When did it happen? It was at the end of summer, just when you returned home to Russia," said the boy.

"I was only five last time I was here in the summer months. That was a long time ago," said Serenity. "Please stop this and release everyone from the ruins," asked Serenity.

"I can release everyone, but you alone have a trial before you leave here. But can we talk more before you go?" asked the boy.

"Yes, we can talk. Just release the others from the ruins," said Serenity.

The boy lifted the spell he used to trap everyone in the ruins. He also lifted the rest of the ruins from beneath the lands. Serenity sits down on floor of ruins tired of standing and hasn't realized how long she been in the ruins. It had been almost a full day since she entered the ruins. She was getting tired, not sure why. She normally could go days without food, but she's also gone almost twenty-four hours without water.

"Boy, why look so sad?" asked Serenity.

"I don't want to be dead anymore," said the boy.

"Why not, what changed your mind?" asked Serenity.

"I want to be with you and be able to hang out again," said the boy.

"I'm sorry I couldn't grant your wish. I would be going against a rule I need to follow," said Serenity.

"Serenity, when have you ever followed the rules and laws?" asked the boy.

"Never, but I need to. I'm trying to reunite my family back together," said Serenity.

"Okay, Serenity, then I will wait for you to return again," said the boy.

"Please don't do that. You would be better moving on than waiting for me," said Serenity.

"I would, but I would like you to play one last game with me," said the boy.

Serenity just then had a vision from the past when she was a child herself. It showed her in these very ruins dressed up as a pirate playing with this boy. They would pretend rocks were gold and that their ship was a big boulder. They fought imaginary enemies in the form of fellow pirates. Serenity looked at the boy with sad eyes after seeing a vivid vision and memories of the past with the boy. The boy disappeared only because he didn't want to see Serenity sad over his death. She couldn't tell if he disappeared or if he actually left the world of the living for good or just to ignore the fact that she was sad over his death.

CHAPTER THIRTY-ONE

NIGHTMARE III FINALLY got out of bed after being stuck in bed for the last three days recovering. It was late in the evening when he got up and got to the bathroom to shower and get dressed for the evening; there was someone he must go and talk to. He was dressed in his royal attire wanting to be taken seriously by the man he was seeking an audience with. The fact that he was even considering to seeking out General Siki, the general that trained all the soldiers. General Siki was well-known for his training methods. He was renowned for the fact he pushed the trainees to their limit and getting them to have their full potential come out. After walking the castle grounds to General Siki's office near the training grounds, he knocked on the door.

Inside General Siki's office, he was sitting at his desk going over training routines. He got up to answer the door when he heard the knock at the door. He stood 6'5". He had a short army haircut. His hair was black with red highlights; he had blue eyes and tan skin. He wore the standard general uniform. The standard general would wear a black uniform with a wing symbol on the upper-left sleeve and a serpent on the upper-right sleeve. The name *General Siki* was on one of the pockets on the left, and on a right pocket was the royal family crescent, which connected in the middle to five crescent moons on each point of a star and black boats.

"My prince Nightmare III, how may I help you?" asked General Siki.

"I would like you to train me to fight," said Prince Dragon III.

"Why should I train you in fighting? It's not a required skill for a prince," said General Siki.

"I want to get stronger because there is a girl I want and be able to protect, but a man stands in my way as her protector," said Prince Nightmare III.

"Fine, I'll train you, Prince Nightmare III, but don't expect me to take it easy on you just because you are royalty," said General Siki.

"That's fine by me. I wouldn't expect anything less from one of our top generals in the Firelands," said Prince Nightmare III.

"Be at the training ground first thing in the morning. That's when your training starts," said General Siki.

"Yes, sir," said Prince Nightmare, taking this seriously.

Nightmare II left General Siki's office happy knowing that he was going to be able to learn how to fight and defend himself better after his training was finished with the general. He went straight back to his room knowing that training for the army recruits started early in the morning, and he was not going to get special treatment being the prince.

***

Scott and Exotic met that night after everyone went to their rooms for the evening. They were planning to sneak out of the castle again. Scott knew he was going to have to leave tomorrow and needed to tell Exotic everything. Exotic led the way to the secret passageway so they could sneak out the same way they did the night before.

"Exotic, can we talk?" asked Scott, sad, knowing he needed to go to meet his sister.

"What is it? You sound sad," asked Exotic.

"I'll need to leave and meet up with my sister. I'll be leaving in the morning after I get up," said Scott.

"But I don't want you to leave me," said Exotic.

"I know, and I promise I will return to you as soon as I can after we bring my parents home," said Scott.

"Okay, I'll wait for you," said Exotic.

"I'll come back safely, I promise," said Scott.

The two of them exited the secret passageway and went into the village to hang out one last time before he leaves to meet up with Serenity. Exotic and Scott were approached by the children of the village wanting to play with them. Exotic started to play with the children right away. Scott sat on a bench watching for now. He was admiring how well she did with the kids. Scott wished he could make her his wife. But to him, she was way out of his league. After a while, he joined Exotic and the kids playing games. As the full moon was high in the sky and the kids were getting exhausted, they decided to leave. Exotic wasn't ready go back to the castle knowing in the morning they will have to say their goodbyes.

Exotic held Scott's hand as they walked back to the castle. Scott was hoping they could spend tonight in his room again one last time. Scott knew he couldn't change fate or what he needed to do, but he could at least take advantage of the time they have together. After they reentered the castle and walked back to Exotic's wing, Scott opened the door to his room and leaned against it to hold it open. He hoped Exotic would take it as an invitation into his room. Exotic didn't hesitate and entered the room. Scott shut the door and joined her in the room. They both got into their night attire. Exotic was in a gown and Scott in his boxers. Scott held Exotic gently as they fall asleep in his guest bed.

CHAPTER THIRTY-TWO

YASHA II TURNED to Cloud and Sasha, needing to make sure they knew to leave and leave Serenity's safe return to him. He didn't need others attacked by the oracle; it was bad enough the oracles wanted to get their hands on Serenity.

"Cloud and Sasha, head back outside where it's safer. I'll go to the temple deep in and make sure Serenity returns safely," said Yasha II.

"Why should we trust you, Yasha II?" asked Cloud.

"Because I am only the one of us that can enter the temple and bring her back if they try to keep her," said Yasha II.

"Why would they keep her? What did you do?" demanded Cloud.

"I guess there's no point in keeping it from you, but she has been mated," said Yasha II.

"When, where, and why?" demanded Cloud.

"Two days ago, at Lord Hathaway's ball. The garden was linked to the temple of oracles. I did it as a promise my father made to Lord Belikov to protect his daughter when she and I came of age," said Yasha II.

"I won't pretend I understand any of this, but I'll trust you'll bring her out safely, and I'll talk to Princess Serenity about this," said Cloud.

"Fine, and if you find out what I'd done wrong, we can settle the matter like man," said Yasha II.

"Sounds good to me. I won't pass judgement on you until after I speak with Princess Serenity," said Cloud.

Cloud and Sasha headed for the exit to the ruins. Yasha II headed deeper into the ruins to the temple of the oracles. Yasha II just hoped he could make sure Serenity can leave the temple after the head oracle finds out she's been mated. Once an oracle is mated, the head oracle never lets them leave until after it's proven that they haven't conceived.

Serenity was heading back toward the entrance of the ruins when she walked into the temple. Just as the boy said, she wasn't able leave without passing through the temple. This was the last place Serenity wanted to end up. She knew what the oracles wanted to do if they can get their hands on her. The last thing she wanted to do was end up in the grip of the oracles and not be able finish her task. The best she can do was hope for Yasha II's promise to protect her, make sure she stayed free from them. As she expected, a male oracle appeared before her. He was tall and had shoulder-length hair that was silver; he had silver eyes and pale skin. He dressed in a gold robe. She's never seen him before, but she was assuming by his appearance he was the Head of Oracles.

"So we finally meet, princess. There's been a lot of talk round the temple about a princess who escaped the temples even though she is an oracle of age," said the head oracle.

"If you know of me, you will be willing to let me go then," asked Serenity.

"No, not exactly, because other rumors have it you have been mated by an oracle recently," said the head oracle.

"I'm not telling you anything. Let me go," demanded Serenity.

"I don't think so. Your kind is rare, being your bloodline is pure," said the head oracle.

Yasha II walked in the temple hearing the head oracle arguing with Serenity. Yasha II walked over to them and stood between the head oracle and Serenity. He knew this looked suspicious but didn't care. His goal was to keep her out of the head oracle's hands like his family promised her father.

"Prince Yasha Vasiliev II, stay out of this, this doesn't concern you," ordered the head oracle.

"If it has to do with you wanting to keep Serenity, it has everything to do with me," snapped Prince Yasha II.

"You are making no sense, Prince Yasha II, unless you are the one that mated her," said the head oracle.

"I was, if you must know, and because of my rank, I also gave her my word she wouldn't be forced to stay here," said Prince Yasha II.

"Fine, I may be Head of Oracles, but I'm not a lord or a prince, so I couldn't order you to keep her here, but if she proves to be carrying and lose the pregnancy, then it is you that will answer for it. Am I understood?" said the head oracle.

"Yes, but I highly doubt that she will, you won't find out without seeking info from another who can tell future and last person that could is currently frozen in crystal and ice," said Prince Yasha II.

"You shut up. Just because we lost Lord Belikov doesn't mean you get to bring him into this," said the head oracle.

"Actually, I do, once you are threating to try to control his only daughter and heir," said Prince Yasha II.

"What the fuck are you talking about? It was said she was lost—that Lord Jonathan killed the whole family," said the head oracle.

"It is true he encased Lord Belikov in crystal and ice, killed him, but he wouldn't kill the only heir to the throne. If anything, it was a rumor spread by Lord Jonathan to hide the children and Lord Belikov's wife," said Prince Yasha II.

"Fine, she can leave," said the head oracle.

Yasha II was relieved he was able to free Serenity from the oracle temple witch, for she alone wouldn't have been an easy task; she would have to try to fight or talk her way out. There would have been some physical stress done to her if she used her magic to try to free herself. Yasha II grabbed Serenity's hand and led her out of the temple and out of the ruins to safety. He knew even though he wanted to warn her about the fact Cloud was going to question her, it was better off not trying to talk and leave the ruins. He was using his magic to keep the rest of the oracles from pulling her back into the temple as they drew farther way from the temple and closer to the exit. There was no way he was allowing another oracle to violate her. He felt guilty enough from what he talked her into letting him do.

As they emerged from the ruins, Serenity noticed both Sasha's and Cloud's worried faces staring at her. She couldn't help but wonder why she was getting all the attention. She knew she was in serious danger after entering the temple, but the spirit wasn't a threat, just a soul of a lost childhood friend. Serenity did not even realize it had been a full day since she entered the ruins. But all she knew was that she was ready to get a drink after going without since she left her uncle's castle and just go on walking and clear her head. Cloud has a look of the fact that he needed a word with her. She knew she couldn't deny him since he was considered a protector of her.

"Cloud, once we return to my uncle's castle and we all get drinks and food, we can talk," said Serenity.

"As you wish, princess," said Cloud, knowing she was right, and he realized then they had gone at least twenty-four hours without food or water.

Yasha II turned to Serenity; he needed to say goodbye because he couldn't be seen at Lord Hathaway's castle. The Hathaways and Capulets couldn't stand his family.

"Serenity, we must part ways," said Yasha II.

"Why, you were at the Hathaway ball, sure enough, you would be a welcome guest," said Serenity.

"I'm far from a welcome guest. If you recall, we were sealed off from the others, and the scenes between Lord Vasiliev I and Lord Hathaway," asked Yasha II.

"I'm sorry for imposing on you. I hope we meet again," said Serenity with sad face and holding back the feeling she never realized was arising in her.

"We shell meet again, but for now, I'll be watching over you from a safe dissentience," said Yasha II.

CHAPTER THIRTY-THREE

YASHA II WATCHED as Serenity and her companions headed back to Lord Hathaway's castle. He wished he could hurry after her, but as fate would have it, their paths separate until she gets on the ship home. He won't allow himself to get caught near the Hathaways. He also had the responsibility to make sure nothing happens to her over the coming months.

Serenity walked back to her uncle's castle in silence, not sure how much Cloud has found out about the events that have passed over the last few days. She wished part of her could forget for her own safety, and part of her wished to stay away from the Hathaway lands, but it's the only safe haven without going back to the villages near the port and the bar she stayed in, even with that rude bartender that worked there. Serenity was lost in thought over all the events that had passed since she first entered Japan. Most of them were unpleasant, but damn, she has recalled few good ones as well. But what puzzled her the most was the fact that everyone that has met with her and have connections to oracles call her Lord Belikov's daughter and heir. That was a mystery she wanted to solve, but that's on for another time. That mystery is for after she reunites her current family before digging into the past.

Before she even realized it, Cloud was holding her by the wrist to make sure she doesn't get lost on the way back to the castle since her mind kept wandering away from what she should be doing. Cloud knew that sometimes Serenity can have visions of the past or future without warning and will be in motion of doing one thing but her mind elsewhere, which was what was going on the whole hour's walk back to the castle. Cloud wished sometimes she could control it and wondered if this was one of those times; she just let it come to her instead of pushing back a vision. He also knew that sometimes she uses it to help process the events that unfolded, and this may be one of those times. He doesn't recall a time when they were growing up together before she became

Lord Jonathan's prisoner when she didn't have a vision, when they were walking back from town after getting caught by the royal guard.

Once they reached the castle and dining hall, Serenity finally came out of it from playing back all the events from being chased from the first bar she went into to mingle and rest to running through the woods and coming out near Nighthowler and meeting a rude bartender and staying the day to rest. Then getting caught in the rain and meeting Sasha in a cave. Then meeting her uncle, then Sasha and she were given a place to stay while she looked for Scott. Then the battle with the vampire hunter at the borders of Firelands, where they met Fang and barely escaped with their lives. Then finally meeting Lord Dragon II, causing a scene. Running into Nightmare III, who reunited her with Scott temporarily. Then a fight breaking out, she returned to her uncle then went to the ball and got mated and finally escaping the ruins, meeting an old childhood friend and getting saved from getting stuck in the oracle realm. She didn't know how she would have ever managed surviving Japan alone being on this long journey so far just to reunite with her brother. She wondered what was to come.

Cloud, Sasha, and Serenity sat down to get some food and water when the hall doors opened, and her uncle came in the dining hall. He looked round seeing that they all came back safely but looked as if they needed to get cleaned up. The three of them had some dust on them that came onto them from spending time in the ruins.

"Good god, does any of you know how to shower before sitting down to a meal?" asked Lord Hathaway, disgusted that they weren't clean for breakfast.

"We are sorry, my lord, we will go at once and get cleaned up before we eat," said Cloud apologetically.

The three of them stood up to leave, feeling ashamed they never even really paid any attention to the fact that they'd gone a whole day without bathing and were down in the dusty ruins. Serenity couldn't help but laugh at getting scolded for being filthy after being in the ruins. It had been so long since she really enjoyed herself or even able to explore the old ruins that she actually forgot her manners when it came to dining in a royal palace. Cloud and Sasha got startled by Serenity's reaction from Lord Hathaway scolding them for going to breakfast filthy.

"Serenity, what's so funny'?" asked Cloud.

"It's just because I've total forgotten royal protocol since I've been searching for my brother and not really had any fun or searching the old ruins where we could end up dirty in a long time," said Serenity.

"Well, let's hurry and get ready for breakfast. We should be meeting your brother soon," said Cloud.

"True, he should be here tomorrow," said Serenity.

Serenity entered her guest room and went straight to the shower. Serenity undressed and turned on the water, keeping an eye on the water temperature. She stood there outside the shower naked wondering if it will be a tough journey home to Russia. Once the water was just right, she stood under it, thinking back to the events that played out in the temple. Man, she disliked that the head oracle was going to try to chain her to that realm. She washed her hair toughly then rinsed out all the soap. Next, she grabbed the conditioner and only did the bottom half of her hair to make it easier to brush out. While she let the conditioner set in her hair, she washed up her body. She couldn't help but think about the night with Yasha II. After she was cleaned and hair was rinsed out of the conditioner, she went back to her room to get dressed. She wished she wasn't trying to pull off this vampire routine, or she'd use magic to clean herself and dress and be done with it all in five minutes.

Once she reentered her room, she noticed a dressed laid out—one of few she brought with her. She decided to wear it just so she wouldn't get in trouble for materializing one here from her closet back home. She then walked out into the hallway, noticing both Cloud and Sasha were ready too. So the three of them went back to the dining hall together. Once they reentered, they noticed that Lord Hathaway just started eating. Serenity wished he wasn't joining them for breakfast, but it was his right to dine with his guests. Lord Hathaway started questioning them on what happened in the ruins, but all they said was that a spirit trapped them all in there until it got what it wanted. They also told him that Serenity was temporarily separated from the group because of a spirit. Cloud and Sasha both failed to tell him a thing to do with Prince Yasha II.

Once they were done with breakfast, Cloud walked Serenity back to her room, needing to talk to her alone. He told Sasha to fall a little behind them but only because she felt it was necessary that she guarded them in the castle. More or less she was only going to make sure no one overheard their contestation.

Cloud, like a gentleman, opened the door for Serenity to her guest room. Serenity walked in first, then Cloud followed behind her. He shut the door. Serenity went and seat on her bed, not sure how long this talk would take, but she was sure it had something to do with Yasha II; the look on Cloud face on not how-to response to what Yasha II said he did to her.

"Serenity, do you know why I want to talk to you?" asked Cloud.

"Yes, I do, and I'll answer your questions you have," said Serenity.

"Good, because it's got a lot for you, princess," said Cloud.

Cloud and Serenity went back and forth on him asking questions and her giving detailed answers. The whole thing lasted a few hours. By the time it was over, Serenity felt like she was being interrogated. She may as well have been, with how much information Cloud wanted out of her. She was hoping Cloud figured out on his own the answer about Yasha II. She was not sure if she should ask what he decided.

"Princess, after what we discussed, I have decided to leave Yasha II alone unless he decided to try to do to you any harm. From what you have told me, it sounds like he was trying to keep you safe from the oracles, even though I'm not 100 percent convinced it's because Lord Belikov asked this of his family," said Cloud.

"I know it sounds a little far-fetched that I'm the daughter of a man encased in ice and crystal for the last thirty years," said Serenity.

CHAPTER THIRTY-FOUR

BACK IN THE Firelands, Scott just got up while Exotic was still asleep. He walked over to the private bathroom in his guest room and turned on the shower. He got undressed while waiting for the water to warm up. He stepped into the warm water to wash his hair and then his body. He wished he didn't have to leave Exotic. But he would be breaking his promise to his family, which would be worse; so for now, he'll leave girl. He wants to do right thing by his family. When he finished, he got out of the shower, walked back to his guest room, and quickly got dressed while Exotic was still sleeping, knowing waking her up and saying goodbye would be harder than disappearing while she was sleeping. He was able to get out of the castle without Exotic waking up and chasing after him. He hoped she can forgive him for leaving her like this. The last thing he wanted to do was see her cry.

Scott had been walking for two hours, and it's early morning; the cafés all over Japan were starting to open up for the day. On his way to his uncle's lands, he decided to stop at one for some breakfast. When he walked in the café, he took a window seat to keep an eye out for trouble coming to the café. After a few minutes of waiting, a waitress came over to the table.

"Sir, can I get you a drink while you look over the menu?" asked the waitress.

"I will take a coffee, please," said Scott.

"Okay, sir, coming right up," said the waitress and walked off to get a fresh pot of coffee.

The time he spent with Exotic was paying off; he could communicate in Japanese with others. He was looking through the newspaper while waiting for the waitress to return with his coffee. He couldn't really read Japanese very well, but he was mostly looking over the photos from events that happened. When the waitress returned a few minutes later with a coffeepot of fresh black coffee, he was ready to order.

"Are you ready to order?" asked the waitress nicely with a smile.

"I would like an order of two eggs over easy, order of bacon, two pieces of french toast, and an order of pancakes," said Scott.

Then the waitress left and put the order in to the chef. Scott went back to looking through the paper and sipping his coffee at the same time. He also was occasionally looking out the window to scan for hunters. Halfway through his meal, the waitress came over with a fresh pot of coffee in her hands.

"Sir, would you like a refill?" asked the waitress.

"Yes, please," said Scott.

The waitress refilled the coffee then left Scott to finish his meal in peace; it was clear to her he wasn't interested in small talk. When Scott was finally ready to leave, she came over with the check, and he handed her money and check back. She went, rang him up, and returned with his change.

Scott got up and left the café. Outside he noticed hunters, but if they noticed him, he wasn't their target, so they let him be. Since Scott was a dhampir, he was easily overlooked by the hunters. He was grateful that hunters don't pay any attention to his kind.

***

Meanwhile back in the Firelands, Nightmare III met up with General Siki, head of training new recruits. The first thing he had them do was run the track a dozen times. Then after that, all recruits were timed on an obstacle course that was set up for both air and land that they had to finish in the quickest time possible, but the catch was they couldn't miss a jump or ring. This course tested the applicants' speed, agility, and attention to detail.

After every applicant finished the course, they were given a partner for the next test. This partner was a member of the guards or army that has been in active duty for at least a year. General Siki was Nightmare III's partner since he wanted to know what the prince was capable of. If any turned out to fail at their sword-fighting skill or magic skills for self-defense, they were dismissed and given a year to improve their skills and try again later; if someone failed three times, they weren't allowed in the royal guard, and depending on exactly what part of the army they wished to join, some of the skills required for a royal guard were not necessary for parts of the army, just goods skill to have. Sometimes a dragon doesn't develop their magic abilities until after their thirties, and the ones that had failed the exam between the ages of eighteen and twenty-nine were allowed at the age of thirty only by recommendation of someone working within the army or royal guard.

General Siki took a personal interest in Prince Dragon III's training. General Siki wanted to know exactly what the young prince was capable of. Once General Siki had a clear understanding of the young prince's weak points in battle, he knew how to help him improve. Even if his prince wasn't looking to join the army at any point soon, these skills will definitely help him out on any one-on-one fight. There may come a time he'd come across a better fighter than himself when finished, but that's really the only way to find out where you needed to work on your skills to improve and beat a strong opponent.

When the rest of the trainees went to lunch, General Siki had Prince Nightmare III stay behind. He wasn't going to allow the prince any lunch until he could last a full minute in a fight with him three times in arow.

"My prince, you need to last a minute or longer three times in row against me before you go to lunch," said General Siki.

"Why is that?" asked Prince Nightmare III.

"Because I need to know you are taking these lessons seriously even though this is day one," said General Siki.

"Okay, if that's what it takes prove to you my heart and mind are fully committed to this training," said Prince Nightmare III.

"It will, and thank you, my prince, for humoring me," General Siki.

"You're welcome, General Siki. I want to prove myself to you and myself anyways," said Prince Nightmare III.

Nightmare III and General Siki practiced over an hour before Nightmare III was finally able to fight in combat for the goal General Siki set. After Nightmare III reached his goal, they broke for lunch themselves.

CHAPTER THIRTY-FIVE

EXOTIC HAD BEEN in her room since Scott left the castle and couldn't decide if she should chase after Scott or stay in her family lands, where she will be safe. She didn't even know if she should care if her father tried to match her with another prince if she decided to stay in her family lands. She also knew leaving it also meant finding out if the Hathaways and the Capulets would accept her for who she really is.

Exotic lay in her bed hoping that Scott will return for her any minute. She was not sure when exactly he left because she woke up to him not in his guest room in the castle and her lying in his bed alone. A few hours have passed by while she was pondering what to do. When all of a sudden, she heard a knock at the door. She got up and rushed over to it, opening it hoping it was Scott, but to her surprise, it was her father. Exotic collapsed from the shock of it being her father and not Scott. Her father, Lord Nightmare Dragon II, picked her up and laid Exotic down on her bed. He sat in a chair next to her bed waiting for her to wake up. It only took her a few minutes to come around.

"Father, how can I help you?" asked Exotic.

"I would like you to meet someone tonight," said Nightmare II.

"Who is he, and why? I know who I want to be with already," said Exotic.

"A nice dragon prince form Ireland," said Nightmare II.

"No, Father, I want Scott," said Exotic.

"But, sweetie, didn't he leave to return home?" asked Nightmare II.

"Yes, but I know in my heart he will come back for me," said Exotic.

"Sweetie, he won't be coming back," said Nightmare II.

Exotic pushed past her father and ran toward the door of her room before Nightmare II recovered. He was startled by his daughter's reaction. Exotic made it out her room and ran toward the front gates to leave the castle, upset with her father. Exotic honestly believed her father was lying to her face about Scott. She returned to the cave they first stayed in together. Exotic sat in the dark cave hoping Scott would come back for her.

Back in Exotic's room, once Lord Dragon II pulled it together, he walked out of her room. He then gathered the royal guard and the soldiers together. When he was sure all of them were in one area, he got their attention on him.

"I want three hundred of you to go out in search of my daughter. She can be anywhere within my lands or the surrounding lands. Find her and bring her home safely," ordered Lord Dragon II.

He then left to go see his wife and tell her of the news about their daughter running off. He wished he could be out with his men searching for his daughter. He hoped his people don't bring her harm once they find out she was outside the castle unguarded. Not all his people cared for the way he ruled or respected the royal family.

CHAPTER THIRTY-SIX

SERENITY WOKE UP next morning after resting from Cloud's interrogation; she was starving even though she ate normally yesterday after returning from the ruins with Cloud and Sasha. She was even experiencing more visions, like dreams, the last few nights since the ball. Serenity's uncle Jason walked in her guest room without knocking to check on her. Serenity went to get up, wanting to get herself food but knowing her uncle would start getting suspicious if it wasn't blood she was after.

Her uncle had a worried look on his face since Serenity had actually been asleep for the last twenty-four hours after dinner last night. Serenity got out of bed, not sure why, but she went weak at the knees, collapsing to the ground, unbale to stand at the moment. Jason caught her, surprised at the fact his niece was weak. He knew she should be able to go without food or water for up to six months.

"Serenity, are you feeling well?" asked Uncle Jason.

"Yes, I'm pretty sure I just overdid it with the use of magic last night and not taking enough food," said Serenity.

"I would still like to have you looked at, Serenity," said Uncle Jason.

"Uncle, that's not necessary. I'll have my doctor take a look at me when I return to Russia," said Serenity.

"Serenity, that wasn't a request but an order for you get looked at," said Uncle Jason.

"Uncle, I don't want to see a doctor. I'm sure that what I have will pass in time," said Serenity.

She was in denial of the truth and didn't want to believe what Prince Yasha II told her to be true. Even if it was true, both the Hathaways and the Capulets can't find out. Both families would hand her over to the oracles without a second thought—what she thought Lord Hathaway would do as well.

Her uncle left the room hoping her brother would be able to convince her when he got there. Lord Hathaway knew the truth about Serenity. He couldn't believe how much she'd grown to represent the late Lord Belikov and his wife. He only had the pleasure of meeting the couple a few times to discuss matters of a truce with him. But the night they were going to finalize the truce, on his way to the Belikov lands from the port, he ran into some of his brother's men.

That night, Serenity's fate changed from the future heir of Belikov lands to his brother's ward. Lord Hathaway knew who the Belikov heir was, but to keep all three of the children that were in the care of the Belikov family, he never revealed the truth about the Belikov bloodline to Lord Capulet. His baby sister was never told the truth either. Her husband was treated as property, and the last thing he was going to do was endanger her with the knowledge of the Belikov heir.

Lord Hathaway knew even if he got her looked at and helped with everything, he'd find out he'd have to stay away from his brother-in-law. He was willing to protect Lord Belikov's heir at any cost, but when it came to his brother-in-law, if she became useless to him or more valuable to another, he would trade her for money. Lord Hathaway knew of Serenity's connection to the oracles since she was five and convinced his brother-in-law to keep her out of Japan; the oracles have more temples in Japan than Russia. On top of that, the Capulets weren't concerned with the oracles, so she was safe in the Capulet lands. The Capulets sealed off the temple and the ruins within their land many years before Serenity became a ward of Lord Capulet.

Lord Hathaway wasn't sure what exactly the Belikovs were but only that their bloodline was of a pureblood. He wished he could help the young princess more, but there was only so much he can do without getting charged with treason against his brother-in-law. The fact his brother-in-law was charging him with treason didn't scare him. The only thing that scared him was the fact that Serenity was being used as a tool for Lord Hathaway or any lord seeking control over the Belikov lands of crystal and ice.

CHAPTER THIRTY-SEVEN

SCOTT FINALLY MADE it to the Hathaway lands and the castle. He was greeted by the royal guard. Scott was surprised when they wouldn't let him pass. This was a sign that Lord Hathaway ordered them to either bring him to him or not let him in at all.

"Sorry, Prince Scott, we were ordered to bring you to Lord Hathaway right away," said one of the guards that stopped him.

"Is something wrong that he requires me to meet with him right away?" asked Prince Scott.

"Sorry, Prince Scott, but we weren't informed," said the guard.

"Fine, take me to my uncle then," said Prince Scott.

The guards did as Prince Scott requested without another word. Once they reached Lord Hathaway's chambers, they knocked on the door.

"Come in," ordered Lord Hathaway.

The guards opened the door and let Prince Scott in the lord's chambers and closed the door behind him. They then returned to their post.

"Uncle, you wished to see me?" asked Scott.

"Yes, it has to do with your sister," said Uncle Jason, concerned for his niece's health.

"Where is my sister, and what happened to her?" demand Scott.

"Watch your tone with me, young prince, this isn't your father's land," warned Lord Hathaway.

"Sorry, Uncle, I'm worried about my sister," said Scott.

"I'm not sure what happened. I couldn't get her to see a doctor," said Uncle Jason.

"Please let me see my sister," asked Scott.

"Okay, I hope you can talk some sense into her to see a doctor before you head back to Russia," said Uncle Jason.

"I won't make any promise, but I'll try to get her to see one," said Scott.

Lord Hathaway showed Scott the way to Serenity's guest room. Lord Hathaway also didn't know what happened to Serenity at the ball or what happened when she got in the ruins and the temples. But he expected something happened to cause her condition. Scott worried about his sister, but he knew she may still refuse medical attention until she meets up with a doctor she trusts. He didn't blame her; his uncle's medical staff were a little iffy when it came to treating her. Once in front of Serenity's guest room, Lord Hathaway knocked on it.

"Come in," said Serenity.

Lord Hathaway opened the door and let Scott go in, and he closed the door and returned to his chambers.

"Brother, what a surprise," said Serenity, sitting up.

"Sister, are you all right?" asked Scott, worried.

"I'll be it just caused from overdoing it last few days. It should pass by time we get on the ship," said Serenity, still not admitting the truth about the events at the ball. She couldn't even tell Cloud everything.

"Sister, you sure you shouldn't be checked over before we leave for the port?" asked Scott, worried about her health.

"Yes, brother, I'm sure everything alright and it be safe for me not having get a checkup until after we get on the ship or home," said Serenity.

Scott was wishing he came sooner; maybe he could have prevented this if he didn't stay a little longer with Exotic. He was feeling guilty for not being here and stopping whatever was causing her to be weak now. Lord Hathaway walked in the room without knock just in case Serenity resting make sure sibling are doing well. He looked to Scott before speaking.

"Scott, don't beat yourself up over the way your sister is. Things would have turned out the same way even if you were here. She's free-spirited. She also has a guardian angel looking out for her to make sure she's safe. What ills her shouldn't kill her," said Lord Hathaway.

"You sure, Uncle?" asked Scott.

"Yes, Scott, she will be fine," said Lord Hathaway.

CHAPTER THIRTY-EIGHT

MEANWHILE, BACK IN the Firelands, everyone was preparing to go to bed except for Prince Nightmare III and General Siki. General Siki and Prince Nightmare III had been at it all day and most of the evening training. Prince Nightmare III knew he only had a small window while Serenity was still here in Japan before she'd leave and head back to Russia. General Siki had high expectations of Prince Nightmare III, so he kept him training longer than the rest of the new recruits. General Siki had Prince Nightmare III's training go into the early hours of morning. It was 2:00 a.m. before they retired for the night, or what was left of it. After only getting six hours of sleep and time to get dressed for the day and have breakfast, General Siki and Prince Nightmare III were training again and would be at it all day, only given an hour for lunch and dinner and two fifteen-minute breaks throughout the training day.

***

Exotic returned to the castle only long enough to get ready to sneak out again. But this time she was going to go in search of Scott, unable to get him out of her mind. Exotic loved him more than anything in the whole world. She wanted to make sure she had a week's supply of clothes before leaving to go after Scott. She knew she also would need her own bathing supplies as well. She even grabbed a few passports she had made with allies that her father couldn't track. She wasn't looking to be found by her own people after leaving the Firelands. She dressed as a commoner to go unnoticed by anyone that would recognize her. As Exotic was leaving the Firelands, the children she plays with at night when she sneaks out approached her wanting to play.

"Sorry, little ones, but I can't play right now. I'm leaving, but once I return home, I'll play again," said Exotic, who was in a hurry to make it out of her father's lands before dawn.

"Promise you will?" asked the children.

"I promise, little ones," said Exotic before leaving her home village behind.

A while later, the maids went in to check if their princess needed anything before they retired for the night. When they opened her room door because they had gotten no answer from knocking on the door, they realized that the princess was missing again. They rushed out the room to notify their lord that the princess was missing. The maid knocked on Lord Dragon II's chambers.

"Come in," said Lord Dragon II annoyed.

The maid walked in wishing she wasn't the one giving the lord the bad news about his daughter's disappearance.

"Speak," ordered Lord Dragon II.

"Your daughter has gone disappearing from her room," said the maid.

"What do you mean my daughter has disappeared!" yelled Lord Dragon II, unable to control his anger.

"She's not in here, my lord," said the maid, scared of his anger.

Lord Dragon II rushed out of his chambers and crossed the castle to his daughter's chambers, wanting to see for himself if what the maid said was true. When he reached her room, he didn't knock on the door, Lord Dragon just opened it. What he found inside was an empty bed still freshly made. Her hairbrush and some of her women's products she kept on her makeup stand were amiss. Lord Dragon II stood there frozen at the sight of his daughter gone. He was hoping she would have been returned to him by guards he sent in search of her safety. But she managed to avoid them. On top of it all, she has managed to return home and take off again.

Lord Dragon II sent all his messengers out to inform the guard to continue looking for the princess and not to bring any harm to her. She was to be returned safely home.

***

It was early morning, and Nightmare III was just getting up and getting ready to start his training with General Siki. Nightmare III wanted to become one of the best when it came to fighting; he would like to stand a chance against Cloud if it came down to them fighting again. He hated how Cloud toyed with him and showed him no mercy. The way Cloud fought as if he was trained from a young age. As he thought about it, he realized Serenity has skills to fight as well, and he didn't understand why. All the guards he met over the years, none of them were female; all were male. Nightmare III realized, at this rate, he won't gain enough fighting skills to match Cloud, so he will need to make the call to still go after her tomorrow or not; they've been training for two days now. Yet he didn't have a clue if Serenity was still in Japan or not. Nightmare III planned to leave and go after her one way or another.

CHAPTER THIRTY-NINE

SERENITY GOT UP and dressed for the day. She went left of her guest room, heading to the dining hall. She needed some more food after a long time in the ruins. As she headed to the dining hall, her uncle came up to her wanting to speak to her.

"Uncle Jason, can I help you?" asked Serenity.

"I want details. What happened, and why?" said Uncle Jason.

"Do I need tell you everything that happened in there? It's a bit of a sore subject," asked Serenity.

"Yes, Serenity, if your father, Lord Capulet, asks me questions and I can't tell him the truth about what happened during your stay here, he could have me killed," said Uncle Jason.

Serenity knew telling him some of what happened in the ruins won't get Prince Yasha Vasiliev II in trouble with the Capulets or the Hathaway lords.

"Fine, but after I get a drink and food," said Serenity.

Serenity went to the dining hall to get some food and something to drink. After being in the ruins, she ate more than normal, and it didn't concern her. The fact they had no food while in the ruins and the fact she barely ate after they returned. Serenity was walking to her uncle Jason's chambers to talk to him about what happened in the ruins. When she was suddenly met by her brother Scott in the hallway.

"Sister, can we please talk? I'm worried about you," said Scott.

"Brother, what are you worried for?" asked Serenity.

"Because the way you are eating lately, it's more than normal for a young vampire," said Scott.

"But I feel perfectly fine," said Serenity.

"Sister, I know I couldn't make you, but please get checked before we leave to head home," asked Scott.

"Sorry, brother, but it will have to wait until we get home. I don't trust the doctors here," said Serenity.

"But, sister, you could be traveling pregnant," said Scott.

"It's a chance I'm willing to take," said Serenity.

"Then promise me you will get checked out when we return home," said Scott.

"I promise I'll be looked at after we return home," said Serenity.

Serenity went to deal with her uncle knowing it's been a week since she and Prince Yasha II mated. She was wondering if her brother was right about his suspicion. She walked in her uncle's chambers and noticed a man talking to her uncle. To her surprise, he has some similar features as she besides the gender difference. Lord Hathaway also able see the spirit. But both the spirits of Lord Belikov and Lord Hathaway didn't notice her as they talked. She was hiding behind one of the pillars in the room.

"Lord Hathaway, I want to see my daughter. We both know your sister, not her mother, Serenity, is a pureblood shape-shifter falcon," said the spirit of Lord Belikov.

"No, Lord Belikov, you are just spirit of dead man," said Lord Hathaway.

Serenity was shocked and couldn't believe she thought the spirit was her father. Serenity slipped past Lord Belikov and Lord Hathaway an in to her uncle's sleeping chambers. Once in there, she lay down. She kept going over it in her mind, thinking she was stupid to think she never spoke to the spirit to find out the truth. There were so many questions running through her mind. When she heard the door shut, it wasn't her uncle. It was Yasha II, after sneaking back into the Hathaway lands and the spirit with which she saw earlier.

Yasha II walked over to Serenity, needing to talk to her.

"Serenity, can we please talk? There are things I would like to know," asked Yasha II.

"Sure, what would you like to know?" asked Serenity.

"Do you have any feelings for me after what we did during the ball?" asked Yasha II.

"I would be in denial if I said I haven't thought about what happened between us. But as for having feelings toward you, I'm not sure how I feel at moment—after everything I've been through," said Serenity.

Serenity was not sure how to tell him about what she suspected was going on with her since she was uncertain.

"Serenity, what's bothering you? I can tell something's worrying you. You can tell me anything. It won't get back to the oracles," said Yasha II.

"Okay, Yasha II. I…may be—" said Serenity and cut herself off after hearing the door open.

Jason walked in the room, but he didn't see Yasha II. Yasha II concealed himself to where only Serenity could see him. Where Yasha II was concealing himself would even prevent people that can see spirits from seeing him. Uncle Jason walked into his room to see Serenity in his bed waiting for him.

"Serenity, you are what, you are only eighteen or nineteen, aren't you?" asked Uncle Jason.

"Nothing that concerns you, Uncle Jason, and I'm in my thirties," said Serenity.

"Who where you talking to?" asked Uncle Jason.

"No one that wants to see you, and they left already," said Serenity, lying about Yasha II having left the castle.

CHAPTER FORTY

BACK IN SASHA and Cloud's room, they waited for news on Serenity. When out of the blue they heard a knock on the door. Cloud got up to answer it and found that it's Yasha II.

"Yasha II, I thought that you have left this land due to the fact that the Hathaways and Capulets don't get along," said Cloud.

"I came back to check on Serenity, and I need to ask Sasha a favor before I leave," said Yasha II.

"Yasha II, what is the favor?" asked Sasha.

"I got to leave for Serenity's safety and would like you stay with Serenity for her safety," said Yasha II.

"I can do that, but why not ask her brother Scott?" asked Sasha.

"Sasha, Scott would kill Yasha II most likely if he found out he was near her," said Cloud.

Then Yasha II walked out to leave the castle. Serenity found Yasha II not wanting to wait until they'd meet again to finish what she was going to tell him or wanting him to leave her. Yasha II noticed her before she got close.

"Serenity, why are you out and about? You should be resting," asked Yasha II.

"We need to finish the conversation we started back in my uncle's room," said Serenity.

"Okay, but please rest after?" asked Yasha.

"Okay, Yasha. I may be pregnant by you after what happened the night of the ball," said Serenity.

Yasha hugged her, happy about the news. But he remembered the promise made to the head oracle.

"Serenity, promise me you won't be reckless and get rest, and if you need me, come for me. You know how to find me. I'll always be there waiting for you," said Yasha.

Yasha II put his necklace that was of his family crest around her neck.

"If you end up crossing any land related to my family, this will grant you and your companion safe passage and sanctuary if necessary. Tell them the crest was gifted to you by me, and I granted you protection until my family can entered to official an alliance with your family later on," said Yasha II.

Yasha II left Serenity to keep her safe. She was trying be strong seeing him go, but as soon as he was out of sight, Serenity broke down and started to cry. Sasha took her wolf form in hopes to comfort Serenity.

"You have become upset with Yasha II leaving you." Serenity started cuddling Sasha like a child with its teddy bear.

CHAPTER FORTY-ONE

SERENITY WOKE UP late that night. She looked around trying to orientate herself. It took a few minutes for her to realize she was in Sasha's guest room.

"Sasha, how did I get here? Last thing I remember was crying in the hallway and cuddling up to you," said Serenity.

"I brought you inside my room after you fell asleep so you could rest comfortably," said Sasha.

Serenity got up but had to lie back down. Serenity's body began to ache, and she remembered what happened between her and Yasha II. The ache was more of a yearning for Yasha II. Scott walked into Sasha's room unannounced and walked up to the bed wanting to talk to Serenity, Sasha, and Cloud.

"Sister, we should leave here tonight. Staying here is not good for your health," said Scott. "When we get home, we can have a doctor check you over before we go after Mother and Father," said Scott.

"But how, brother? I can't move on my own at the moment," said Serenity.

"You silly girl. You got Cloud, Sasha, and I to help you," said Scott.

"Okay, we will leave tonight, brother," said Serenity.

Little did Scott know, Fang and Yasha would join them. Yasha would join them only if Serenity would go to him. Serenity didn't have to leave wherever she was to reach Yasha II, only to open up a portal to the oracle realm. Serenity was not sure how she felt about Yasha II. She thought of Fang as a true friend and trusted him. She knew she didn't love him anything beyond a friend or brother. Serenity knew it would be wise to build a relationship with Yasha II. Cloud decided to take Serenity first, knowing he could get her out unseen with the others with him. When they got to the gate, they were stopped by the guards.

"We have to go on a mission to make sure the one that was with Serenity has left the castle," said Cloud.

"Okay, Cloud," said the head guard, allowing them to pass, unable to tell that Cloud was lying to him.

When Cloud knew it was safe, he removed the spell from Serenity and him. Cloud was unofficially known as the leader of the group when Fang was not around.

"Serenity, how are you feeling? We are still a ways from being safely outside Lord Hathaway's lands and can see him again," said Cloud.

"I'm feeling fine," said Serenity.

"Cloud, who exactly are we meeting?" asked Scott.

"Fang and Yasha II. I also think Yasha II may have got her pregnant," said Cloud.

"Cloud, let one of us carry Serenity so you can have a break from it and rest your arms and back," said Sasha.

"Fine, which one of you wants a turn? She's not as light as she looks, or you may think she is," said Cloud, warning Scott and Sasha.

Serenity slapped Cloud for his comment. Scott then picked up his sister Serenity and started walking with Cloud and Sasha, not even breaking a sweat keeping up with them.

CHAPTER FORTY-TWO

BACK IN THE Firelands, Exotic was preparing to leave, wanting to see Scott again, missing him. Where she was a dragon shape-shifter, she had the ability to track people. Exotic packed enough clothes to last her awhile and a mix of clothes; most of them made her look like a commoner or a noblewoman. Exotic took with her all the money she had been saving up over the many years. She took her passport to make sure she didn't get in trouble for traveling to other countries along her journey to find Scott. Exotic left her parents a letter to find later after she was gone. Exotic traveled one las time to the secret passage she used to escape the castle one last time. She left through the door one last time without looking back, knowing one day she will finally return to the castle.

The guards weren't yet guarding the area where she slipped out through the secret passageway. She grew up in this castle and was at one point put under a spell to remain in deep sleep for three thousand years, waiting for her mate to be born. She was under the spell from age one until her mate was a year old. Little did Exotic know was that Serenity used to visit the sleeping dragon that was unhatched.

Serenity already knew the destiny of Exotic. Serenity also knew of a Dragon that was fated to be Exotic's mate. Exotic's fate was intertwined with Serenity's from the beginning. Serenity also knew this had to do with her. Exotic's fate was tied to another Belikov line that wasn't related to Serenity's family. This Belikov family was not from land earth at all but from another world entirely. But Exotic herself wasn't from earth either. She wasn't even related to the Dragon family that raised her. But Lord Dragon was a family friend of her father's. Due to the fact Serenity's looks are that of age thirty didn't mean she actually was that young; her own family lines had a secret of their own. But the fact remained that Serenity and Exotic will be related by marriage one day.

Exotic reached the end of the secret passageway and exited and noticed the children waiting for her.

"Princess, can we play tonight?" asked the oldest child, only age six.

"Sorry, but I must leave for a while. Please be good," asked Exotic.

"Okay, we will, princess," said the children.

She left the children with a smile. Exotic was heading for the Hathaway lands, not knowing that they have already left and were heading to the port to meet up with Captain Mason, a friend of Serenity.

CHAPTER FORTY-THREE

CAPTAIN MASON AND his crew were heading back to Japan as part of his normal route between Japan, Russia, China, and America. He was also hoping to see Princess Serenity and help her some more. Captain Mason was a loyal friend to Princess Serenity and the Belikov family and would help them out when they needed it and he was nearby. He would especially help Princess Serenity, whom he has a crush on. Captain Mason's ship was thirty minutes away from Japan, if the weather stayed good, but as a ship captain, he knew Mother Nature can change at a drop of a dime. Once they reach port, they will have a twenty-four-hour break before heading to Russia. This break was to refuel and resupply along with picking up new passengers and letting some off. He knew Serenity was here in Japan and was not sure if she was ready to depart Japan to return home to Russia yet. Captain Mason retired to his captain's quarters after his first mate took over. Captain Mason wasn't in his quarters no more than fifteen minutes when he was disturbed by the weather. There were storm clouds coming in from the west, and fast. Captain Mason took a hard right off course and away from the storm to come back toward the port. This took a good hour to avoid the storm and to dock in the port of Japan. Captain Mason got lucky to be able to dock at the same place he let Serenity off two months earlier.

SPEAKING THE TRUTH AND BRINGING HOME JONATHAN AND JANINE

CHAPTER FORTY-FOUR

SCOTT, SASHA, CLOUD, and Serenity were almost at the port in Japan, where Serenity was let off in Japan two months earlier. Serenity decided to walk on her own when they got to the port hoping to see Captain Mason's cruise ship. She wanted to see her friend and see if he can help her get to China and was not sure what his ship schedule was. She started heading to where in the port Captain Mason's cruise ship was when he dropped her off.

"Serenity, where are you going, and why are you so excited?" asked Scott.

"I'm hoping a friend has returned back to Japan," said Serenity.

Serenity was walking through the port looking at all the ships that have come in. The port had six bays. The ports had several entrances to the port where the ships were, and Serenity knew that there was a process to go through before boarding Captain Mason's ship. They started with the security checkpoints. They all were able to get past the checkpoint, but they still had to check in to board the ship on dock to sail to Russia. Serenity and her companions were given directions to which line to check in for Captain Mason's ship. Once they reached where they needed to be to check in, they noticed that it wasn't that long, so they broke up in two groups based on the number of people to each of the five rooms they have. Since Serenity, Yasha II, and Fang were in single rooms, they went first to check in since the process would be a bit quicker with them. Cloud, Sasha, Scott went next even though Exotic hasn't caught up with them yet. Scott knew there's still time before boarding stopped, for her to get on the ship. The group sat together while waiting to board the ship. Since Serenity did the purchases online, the group was able stay together on the ship, and she was able to use funds from her account and not worry about being tracked to the ship. She whipped her hard drive and left the computer at her uncle Jason's castle, planning on replacing it once she returns to

Russia. After an hour of waiting to begin boarding the ship, Serenity and her companions were one of the first to board the ship. They walked up the long ramp to deck 7, where everyone was boarding the ship. Serenity and Yasha II were keeping it secret on what happened between them back at Lord Hathaway's castle. Serenity fought the urge to show any affection toward Yasha II.

When on the ship and waiting to set sail, Serenity decided to really explore the ship after getting her stateroom prepared. She couldn't believe she made it this far on reuniting her family. She also learned more about herself and past than she could ever imagine. She also torn between wanting the full truth and not sure how she going to achieve that. She set aside all her feelings and decided to enjoy the journey back home to Russia with her family and friends. She hoped that it's false that she was possibly pregnant by Yasha II. She took the time she had before they set sail to find out what was all on the ship. Serenity explored all the levels that were open to the guests on board.

Serenity knew they would be at sea for about a week before hitting the shores of Russia. Serenity knew she may be putting all the rest of the passengers and the crew in harm's way if the Vampire Hunter Society found out her location or started attacking ships at random in search of her and her family. She wished there was another way around this burden she was putting on Captain Mason for assisting her. Serenity knew that this risk would come to any ship crew or airline crew if she chose to fly. The one thing that was certain was on the ship, they could escape if needed. The ship was the only way her companions and she could escape with their lives if it came down to it.

CHAPTER FORTY-FIVE

HOURS AFTER SERENITY and her companions left the Hathaway lands, Exotic, Scott's princess friend, finally reached the lands. Exotic hoped Scott was still there because she knew what she was risking by coming to the Hathaway lands. She knew her father didn't care for Russians, yet he took a liking to Scott. Exotic wished she didn't let him leave without her. After walking through the Hathaway lands and making it to the castle, she was able get in with no hassle, but she found herself face-to-face with Lord Hathaway.

"What is a Firelands princess doing here in my castle? You are not part of my family," demanded Lord Hathaway.

"I am looking for Scott Capulet. He said he was coming here," answered Exotic.

"He and his sister are missing. I'm assuming they are heading back home to Russia at this point," said Lord Hathaway. "Guards," called Lord Hathaway.

Exotic got nervous that he was going bring harm to her. The guards surrounded Princess Exotic.

"Escort her out of my castle. No harm is to come to her," ordered Lord Hathaway.

He then left toward his chamber, vanishing around the corner of the hallway.

Exotic was safely escorted out of the castle, and no harm came to her from his guards. She started walking toward the port knowing it was still a ways off and day has broken; the sun has risen in the sky. She didn't realize it was the early hours in the morning when she got to the castle; she wasn't paying any attention that the darkness of night was fading before she went inside and was confronted by Lord Hathaway.

Exotic hoped that by the time she makes it to the port that they were still there. If not, she knew where they were going and will travel by other means. She wanted to try to make it before they shut down access to the ship before it set sail. She knew if she flew, she would make it in time, but she was trying to keep her identity a secret, so she travelled by foot. She refused to use her horse because it would have been recognizable along with any other means of transport.

CHAPTER FORTY-SIX

BACK AT THE ship, it was about to set sail back to Russia, where most of them were from but Cloud, who was from Finland. Serenity has been wandering the ship and found the captain's control room. But the crewman outside refused to let her see the captain. Instead of fighting with the crewman, she went and sat on floor outside the captain's quarters. But before he even showed up, she fell asleep on the floor outside the captain's quarters. Twenty minutes later, while she was fast asleep, Captain Mason showed up. He opened up the door to his quarters and then picked up Serenity and carried her into his room and laid her on his bed. He made up bed for himself on the floor to get rest as well. After an hour or so, Serenity woke up seasick. Captain Mason woke up to the sound of Serenity being sick. This made him grow concerned for her safety.

"Serenity, what's the matter?" asked Captain Mason, worried.

"I'm not sure. I have suddenly become sick," said Serenity.

"Okay, I'll get the doctor on staff to see what he can do," said Captain Mason.

Captain Mason left Serenity in his private quarters while he walked to the sick bay of the ship to get a doctor to see Serenity. He was not sure what made her fall ill, but he knew that her kind don't get sick easily; for her to become ill at sea seemed weird to him. He knocked on the door to be polite and made sure the doctor was not with a patient.

"Come in," said the man behind the door.

Captain Mason opened the door, seeing the doctor was sitting at a desk. It was quite in sick bay that doctor only have seen patients that had sea sickness and most of ones he treated never been on ship before.

"Captain Mason, how may I help you?" asked the doctor on board.

"I would like you to come with me and take a look over Princess Serenity, please," asked Captain Mason.

"Okay, Captain Mason, lead the way," said the doctor.

CHAPTER FORTY-SEVEN

BACK IN THE Firelands, Nightmare III finished his combat training with General Siki. The two of them decided to go out to dinner. General Siki knew even though Prince Nightmare III was training, he still feared this training wasn't enough to beat any really experienced fighter like Cloud and Fang, two of his greatest rivals; and both were at least falcon or part falcon. Fang was someone who was in love with Serenity, and Cloud was her protector. After the two of them had dinner outside the castle in a restaurant, they headed back to the castle. Nightmare III was planning to leave without telling his parents that he was planning to go after Serenity. Nightmare III knew his sister has already left the castle for her own reasons already.

When Nightmare III entered the dining hall to be polite and sit down with his family for dinner, even though he'd already eaten. He quickly realized his sister Exotic was still missing.

"Nightmare III, son, have you seen your sister Exotic?" asked Nightmare II.

"No, Father, I got back from the training grounds late last night. I assumed she had gone to bed already," said Nightmare III.

"That's not like you not checking up on your sister," said Nightmare II.

"I have been overtired the last couple of days, been training with General Siki, wanting to improve my skills," said Nightmare III.

"My son, are you planning to leave home now?" asked Nightmare II.

"Yes, Father, I will keep an eye out for my sister while I am gone," said Nightmare III.

"Sounds good, my son, you are dismissed and may leave now," said Nightmare II.

Nightmare II went to his daughter Exotic's room to look for clues on where his daughter could have gone. Inside her room, he found a letter sitting on her bed. It was addressed to him and his wife; the outside of the letter said "Mom and Dad." The front and the back had her official seal signed to her by her father. He picked up the letter and opened it to read it.

> Dear Mom and Dad,
>
> I'm sorry to do this to you but I couldn't ignore my feelings for Scott. I know how much you dislike Russians of any kind. I love him dad and I hope you can understand where I am coming from. I will return home someday hopefully with Scott at my side. I want to get know him and his sister more. I know she looks scary and dangerous to us, but I believe she may have a heart of gold. But you didn't give her a chance dad. I love you mom and dad.
>
> Sincerely,
> Exotic Fireheart Dragon

After finishing reading the letter, Nightmare II got furious, stormed out of his daughter's room, slamming the door behind him. He walked down to his private library to read a bit and blow off some steam from his daughter's goodbye letter before telling his wife what he found out about their daughter.

CHAPTER FORTY-EIGHT

BACK ON THE cruise ship, Scott was standing on the upper deck looking back toward Japan, when he spotted a dragon flying toward the ship. Once the dragon got close enough in view and was starting to descend toward the ship, Scott realized it to be Exotic. But he didn't get why she was out here. As she got closer to the ship, she transformed into a human form with wings coming from her back to make the landing on the ship easier and so she didn't break anything on deck. Once she landed, she pulled her wings into her back. This made her look like a human with long black hair, golden eyes, and tan skin. She also dressed down from a royal attire. Exotic looked at Scott relieved to find him.

"I finally found you," said Exotic, relieved.

"Why did you come after me?" asked Scott, not knowing Exotic's feelings for him.

"I love you and want to get to know you and your sister," said Exotic.

"Okay, I will take you to my room here on the ship, where we can get to know each other better," said Scott.

"Okay, sounds good to me," said Exotic.

Scott started to lead Exotic to his guest room from the upper deck of the ship so they can have some privacy.

Yasha II joined Serenity in Captain Mason's quarters. Yasha II entered through his magic so no one would know he was there. Yasha II held Serenity close while they were alone. He was considered an enemy of the Capulets. Serenity fell asleep in his arms feeling safe. Serenity didn't consider that she was spending time with an enemy of the Capulets and what it may cost her later. Yasha II disappeared sensing Captain Mason outside the door. Captain Mason walked in his quarters with the doctor to see Serenity asleep. He walked over her to wake her up.

"My princess, it's time to wake you, a doctor's here to see you," said Captain Mason.

"Captain Mason, was someone here?" asked Serenity, confused why it's Captain Mason waking her up.

"No, you were alone when I left. No one should have been able to enter my room without a key," said Captain Mason.

"I could've sworn I wasn't alone when I slept," said Serenity.

"Princess Serenity, please let the doctor look you over, and we can discuss this matter after," said Captain Mason.

Captain Mason stepped off to opposite side than what doctor would need. The doctor had what looked like a large briefcase. The doctor set it up to look Serenity over. He brought both a small and a large case. The small one had all his normal supplies a doctor needed; the large one was about forty pounds. The large one contained a portable ultrasound machine. The captain never told the doctor that this patient wasn't human. Captain Mason couldn't risk giving away Serenity's identity to anyone onboard his ship. The doctor did his ultrasound on the assumption that Serenity was human.

Serenity didn't want the doctor to know what she was; most of her companions didn't know what creature she truly was. Serenity knew she couldn't hide anything from Yasha II or Captain Mason. She could try, but it would fail; both of them were able to tell when she was lying. Serenity feared what the doctor might find.

The exam didn't take long at all, thirty minutes at most, and she was nervus through the whole thing, hoping he wouldn't find anything. The doctor looked at her and then to Captain Mason before speaking.

"Captain Mason, I fear that I can't confirm anything, but to be on the safe side, I'll give her something to help with seasickness and also be safe to take just in case she is pregnant. You may want a doctor that knows her better and has better equipment to take a look at her after you hit the next port before letting her travel to sea again," said the doctor.

"I'll keep that in mind, but I'm not going that far inland when we dock next, so it will be up to her," said Captain Mason.

The doctor cleaned his equipment and packed it up to head back to his chambers and turned to Serenity to address her.

"Miss, make sure you get checked when you return to Russia, and if possible, avoid sea travel, or have your doctor get you meds for seasickness, but as far as any onboard records, you've never been treated for seasickness before," said the doctor.

"You are right, as many times I have traveled, it's the first time I've gotten seasickness," said Serenity.

"I won't be able to stop traveling for a while. I'm only temporarily returning home. There are still others I need to find for my family and bring home. My journey won't be over any time soon."

"I understand, but you must think about yourself first. If you give me some personal information, I could possibly give you an answer," said the doctor.

"Thank you, but I'll wait until I see my private doctor to find out the truth," said Serenity.

"As you wish, miss," said the doctor.

He then headed for the door to return to his private quarters for some rest, hoping it stays a peaceful trip. The doctor will be serving with the captain's crew for another two months, then he will have to decide if he's going to go into private practice or take a contract with a hospital of his choosing.

CHAPTER FORTY-NINE

FANG GOT LONELY knowing Serenity was with Prince Yasha II, who was also an enemy of the Capulets. He knew that he couldn't compete with him in her eyes. So to shake the loneliness and longing for Serenity's attention, he walked around the ship not sure where he was going to end up. Fang went as high as he could on the ship and started looking round to see what was going on up on the deck of the ship. Fang noticed Nightmare III flying toward the ship. Fang took to the air knowing what Nightmare III was now. Fang refused to let Nightmare III get anywhere or get his hands on Serenity or anywhere near her. Fang knew Serenity has been different since her uncle Jason's lands.

Fang was willing to fight Nightmare III to keep Serenity safe. Nightmare III was in his full dragon form, and Fang could only fly by bringing out his wings. In a fight, Nightmare III as a full-fledged dragon gave him the upper hand. In a desperate attempt to keep Nightmare III away from Serenity, he took out his secret weapon without knowing the damage it can do to a dragon. The weapon he took out, only Serenity knew what it can do; and being so, she never stayed in firing range of it and let him fire it where innocent people would be harmed. Fang made sure no ships were close enough to be caught in the crossfire of his weapon.

Nightmare III knew he could be in trouble, but he was not sure what Fang's weapon could do for damage. He started breathing fire at Fang, trying to kill him, but Fang was too fast for him, so Nightmare III kept missing his target. Fang was not sure how Nightmare III had become a better fighter but was certain that it won't stop him from killing this dragon.

Serenity was finally able to get up and move after the doctor was done looking her over and gave her medicine; what he gave her had started taking effect. Serenity decided to leave Captain Mason's quarters to go meet up with her companions. Serenity could sense some fighting going on nearby and hoped Fang or Yasha II were not picking a fight with someone special; if it's Nightmare III, she would hate to see him die. She knew he may not even be alive now if he fought with them. Serenity was hoping to run into anyone as she wandered the ship but didn't; when she got on the top deck, she started looking around and decided to look in the air to see if she could see anyone or one of her friends taking a break and stretching their wings.

CHAPTER FIFTY

FANG WENT TO end the fight with Nightmare III. Nightmare III noticed another dragon and a vampire with wings approaching them from the ship. Fang noticed Serenity flying toward them and still wanted to make sure to end it with Nightmare III dead or at least in a state to make him give up on coming after Serenity as a lover.

Serenity noticed Fang in the air fighting but at first didn't notice Nightmare III. Once she noticed Nightmare III, Serenity got scared what Fang was going to do, recognizing the weapon he had out. She flew at Fang and grabbed his arm to try stop him from killing Nightmare III. Fang struggled and tried to set off the weapon. Nightmare III's sister Exotic grabbed him and got between him and Fang.

"Brother, please leave the girl alone and return home. I don't want to see my brother killed," said Exotic.

"Fine, sister, since I don't want to see you sad," said Nightmare III.

Nightmare III started flying back toward his homeland while Serenity struggled with Fang to keep Nightmare III from being killed by him. Cloud, followed by Sasha, came up on the deck sensing Nightmare III around. Sasha wanted to make sure Cloud didn't start something even though she was not sure how she could stop Cloud. Nightmare III and Fang looked at each other realizing the fighting will be pointless at this time since all the girls won't let them finish off Nightmare III. Exotic stayed between her brother and the man that wanted to kill him while he escaped. Serenity used magic to create barrier in front of Cloud and Sasha, restricting them to the ship. She also kept a tight grip on Fang, keeping him from killing both siblings just to finish off Nightmare III.

After Fang, Exotic, and Serenity landed back on the ship, everyone went to their rooms. Fang grabbed Serenity and started leading her back to his room. Exotic went to find Scott and stayed with him. Sasha turned to Cloud and spoke.

"Cloud, it's funny the way Fang is acting. Do you think something is going on between them?" asked Sasha.

"If I had guessed, I'd say he's in love with her, but it may only be one-sided, but only time will tell, but we must protect her," said Cloud, serious like a brother.

CHAPTER FIFTY-ONE

NIGHTMARE III SUCKED up his pride and decided to return home for now. He must let his father know that Exotic was safe and with Scott. He was convinced his younger sister was safe with Scott.

Nightmare III noticed a ship moving toward the cruise ship and recognized one of the vampire hunters on board, and vampire hunters thought Serenity was a dangerous vampire that shouldn't be alive. They didn't like any vampires with strong abilities that were not under their control of the Vampire Hunter Society. Nightmare III found this out by reading one of their minds. Nightmare III went after the vampire hunters in his dragon form hoping to stop them and take them out to protect Serenity, even though no one wanted him near her. The vampire hunter started attacking the dragon that went after them and panicked when their attacks failed, and their weapons weren't made to kill a dragon shifter while in dragon form. Nightmare III set their ship ablaze so the hunters couldn't follow Serenity, the one he loves. All the hunters jumped ship knowing only dragon hunters have the ability and proper weapons to kill a dragon.

Serenity didn't want anything to do with Fang at the moment and wanted be with Yasha II, but due to the fact that no one can know what happened between them, Yasha II kept his distance from her while she was around others but was warned to protect her from harm and any male oracle that may want her. Serenity knew that she couldn't have Yasha II openly right now. She also had a feeling she won't be escaping Fang and return to her room to be able to have Yasha II to herself. So Serenity just stayed with Fang even though it wasn't what she wanted. Fang held Serenity close even though it was not what she wanted. He wanted to keep her safe; he was also worried what Scott, Janine, and Jonathan would do after finding out her secret and who was the father of Serenity's pregnancy. He also knew that he can't go to her family lands with her because if he tried to, he would be thrown in prison for entering her family lands or getting close to the castle for trespassing. The two families were enemies.

"Fang, what's wrong?" asked Serenity. She sensed that something was bothering him.

"It is nothing since it's out of everyone's control," said Fang.

"Like what?" asked Serenity, oblivious that it was about being near her and going to prison for having anything to do with an enemy or just outright kill him.

"Serenity, you know I and Yasha II couldn't enter you family lands without being imprisoned or put to death if found out," said Fang.

Serenity cried at the thought of not being able to have Yasha III near her. But even though he was not visible to people around her due to the risk.

"Serenity, please calm down, you'll be okay. I'm sure we can figure out a way for me and Yasha II to return home with you, so you are safe," said Fang.

"How are you going to do that?" asked Serenity.

"We will figure a way out to be at your side," said Fang.

Fang froze in time, and Serenity was pulled into attritive dimension. She recognized Yasha II right away and went to him.

"Yasha II, what are you doing here? Where am I?" asked Serenity.

"I know you wanted me, and I need to talk to you," said Yasha II.

"Okay, what about Fang?" asked Serenity.

"I will be with you no matter where you go. Being an oracle, I'm able to move freely about. I can come to you anywhere and anytime," said Yasha II.

"Will you be freezing everything around you every time?" asked Serenity.

"No. I could've come in here and shown myself to Fang if I wished, but I want you to myself without a meaningless fight with that falcon," said Yasha II.

"You know all you have to do is come to me and tell me you want me to yourself, and we go somewhere alone even if everyone is against us," said Serenity.

"Then leave him," said Yasha II.

"Okay, after you release the spell on this room," said Serenity.

Yasha II did as Serenity requested and released the room from his spell, and he returned to his own room.

Serenity got up and out of Fang's arms and went to see Yasha II. She headed for the door to leave the room and head back to speak to Captain Mason. She walked across the ship to the control room in hopes of speaking with Captain Mason. As she was walking through the decks to make it back to the control rooms, she was greeted by Captain Mason's first mate. She recognized him from the first trip from Russia to Japan, but she also traveled back to Russia with them at the ship she originally took from Scotland home had been sunk by vampire hunters, and they escaped on to lifeboats and were rescued by Captain Mason's crew.

"Captain Mason wants to speak with you, Serenity Capulet," said the first mate.

"Okay, I was heading to see him anyways," said Serenity.

"Then let me escort you to the captain," said the first mate.

"Okay, thank you," said Serenity.

Serenity was walking to the ship's control room escorted by the first mate to speak with Captain Mason. Serenity knew that even though they were on the ship, they weren't out of the high waters, yet they haven't yet docked in Russia and were heading to China to find her parents yet. The first mate knocked on a door.

"Come in," said Captain Mason, preparing the ship to leave port soon since he needed to check on the equipment while they waited for boarding to finish.

"Captain, I brought Serenity, like you wanted," said the first mate.

"Okay, you finish preparing to leave while I take Serenity to a private area to speak with her," said Captain Mason.

"All right, Captain, leave it to me," said the first mate.

Captain Mason stepped outside the control room. He saw Serenity standing there.

"Thank you for waiting, please follow me, Princess Serenity," said Captain Mason.

"Okay, Captain Mason, lead the way," said Serenity.

Serenity and Captain Mason made it to a private conference room. Serenity sat down knowing that this may last for a while since she asked a lot of the captain so far, and the captain asked nothing of her in return. She was not sure what Captain Mason was after. Captain Mason sat across from Serenity.

"Captain Mason, what did you need?" asked Serenity.

"I want to know if you are feeling any better," asked Captain Mason, concerned for her safety.

"I'm feeling a lot better, thank you for asking," said Serenity.

"We will be making a stop at Paradise Island to drop people off and resupplying on doctor supplies. It's part of our itinerary before continuing to China," said Captain Mason.

"That's fine. I just need to find my parents and bring them home, but I'm nervous about doing that," said Serenity.

"Is it because you're pregnant?" asked Captain Mason, assuming that was the case since she got seasick, but it didn't happen the last time she traveled on the cruise ship.

"A little, but it's nothing I can't handle since I'm not going tell them anything right away," said Serenity. "How did you figure it out? The doctor of the ship never said it. It was only that he couldn't tell for sure if that was the case," asked Serenity.

"I've never seen you so close to any man as you are with Yasha II when away from your brother," said Captain Mason.

"Please keep this to yourself. If my family finds out, it will cause a lot of trouble for Prince Yasha II," asked Serenity.

"I will, my princess," said Captain Mason.

After finishing speaking with Captain Mason, she got up and left feeling relieved about him keeping her secret. Scott couldn't find out about her pregnancy or that Yasha was the father of it.

CHAPTER FIFTY-TWO

IN CHINA, JANINE had been working as a security at a five-star casino. Janine was fast on her feet, and no one argued with her when she asked them to leave the casino. Janine could handle someone twice her size with little effort. Jonathan, her husband, who didn't know how work the tables, got trained to do bartending. Jonathan and Janine always worked the same shift while at the casino. This also allowed her to always protect Jonathan even if they weren't always in exact proximity of each other.

One day, after having the same job for a year, while getting ready for work, Jonathan came up behind his wife and grabbed her to surprise her. Janine jumped and went to attack the one that grabbed her.

"What's the matter, baby girl, does someone not like being surprised?" asked Jonathan.

"No, I don't, specially in my line of work," said Janine.

"Aw, love, don't be such a killjoy," said Jonathan.

Janine threw him down onto the bed and kissed him to shut him up. Janine went and tried to get ready for work. Jonathan lay there surprised she caught him off guard. Janine walked out of the room, leaving her husband all alone stunned in bed. Jonathan went back to bed, not having to work for another four hours.

CHAPTER FIFTY-THREE

SERENITY WENT TO Captain Mason's private quarters and decided to get some rest until the ship docks in Russia. Serenity knew that she still needed to see her doctor about what was going on with her and confirm it with her doctor what the ship doctor suspected. Serenity also knew that she only has a brief time to return to her family castle, restock on emergency funds, and make it back to the ship before Captain Mason deports to Paradise Island and China.

Serenity started heading up to the deck. Yasha II, Fang, Sasha, and Cloud were not far behind her. Yasha II was keeping his hands to himself so he doesn't get caught by Scott. When they got on deck, they were met by Captain Mason.

"Serenity, you have three days to make it back here. That's how long we have to refuel, restock, and give the crew a break," said Captain Mason.

"Okay, Captain Mason. How long will it take for you to return and set sail to China if I miss the ship in three days?" asked Serenity.

"It will be a month's time before I return here and do another run to China," said Captain Mason.

Serenity knew she must make it back in time to set sail with the ship in the next three days. She and her companions disembarked the ship. Serenity, Scott, and their companions walked to the woods. She whistled, and a pure white horse came up to her excited to see her master.

"Good girl, Icicle," said Serenity, praising her horse Icicle.

Icicle started galloping around her master. Serenity walked up to Icicle and patted her, and Icicle limitedly calmed down. Serenity got on Icicle and started riding her toward her family castle. Serenity never uses bridles, saddles, or whips on her horse. Icicle was a companion to Serenity, and she didn't want to use anything on her that may harm her. Serenity liked to keep the natural look to her horse. Icicle looked like a wild horse since Serenity didn't add any extras onto her horse. Serenity had Icicle since she turned sixteen. Serenity loved riding Icicle every day and didn't know what she would do if she were to lose her and didn't want to think about that.

Cloud, Fang, Yasha II, Scott, Sasha, and Exotic followed Serenity by air until mile out from the castle. Cloud was carrying Sasha, Exotic was carrying Scott, Fang and Yasha II weren't carrying anyone. Yasha II was flying right above Serenity, invisible to everyone, and Fang was flying a little lower than Cloud, and Exotic was looking out to make sure they didn't get too close to the Capulet castle and get shot at by a guard standing guard on the towers and walls. Where they got land so far out, it took them longer to reach the castle than Serenity since they would have to walk the rest of the way.

Serenity was greeted by General Charles.

"Welcome back, Princess Serenity, are you done bringing your family home?" asked General Charles.

"No, Scott's the only one returning home and will be along shortly with my friends," said Princess Serenity.

"Okay, I'll tell the castle-guards to be on the lookout for Prince Scott and your friends and tell them not to stop them from entering. My princess, please retire to your room, you look exhausted from your trip," said General Charles.

"Have my doctor meet me there by the time I get up. I'm not staying long. I still have to go after my parents," said Princess Serenity.

"Yes, my princess," said General Charles.

After twenty minutes of walking, Scott, Exotic, Cloud, Sasha, Fang, and Yasha all made it to the castle.

"Prince Scott, who do you bring home with you beside Cloud only one I know you?" asked General Charles.

"These are my sister's and my companions and friends. This is Exotic, Sasha, and Fang," said Scott since he didn't see Yasha II with them.

"I'm sorry, my prince, but your friend Fang will have to leave or be our prisoner in the dungeon," said General Charles.

"Please, just this once, for my sister's sake," asked Prince Scott.

"I'm sorry, my prince, your father would have my head if I let an enemy of the family inside unchained," said General Charles.

"Scott, it is fine, just take care of your sister for me," said Fang.

"Fang, do you dare leave knowing you're one of the few my sister trusts to protect her?" asked Scott, not knowing what exactly was going on with his sister.

"Fine, but how do you suggest I get near her to do that?" asked Fang.

"Good point, since my sister would go off the deep end seeing you in chains," said Scott.

"I'll find a way still to protect your sister no matter what," said Fang.

Everyone had forgotten Yasha II was around due to his magic concealing him from his companions. All of a suddenly, they heard a female screaming from inside the castle.

"That's Serenity," yelled Yasha II, recognizing her voice, blowing his cover.

Yasha II ran past General Charles and Scott, revealing himself. He knew the risk of being the enemy of the Capulets but not an enemy of Serenity's true bloodline.

"General Charles, get my sister's doctor here now," demanded Scott.

General Charles got on the phone at once, calling the doctor.

"Hello," answered a female doctor, even though it was early in the morning and woken up to the cell phone going off.

"I need you to see Princess Serenity Capulet right away, please," said General Charles.

"Okay, I'll be right there," said the doctor; before she was able to get off the phone, she heard Princess Serenity screaming in background.

The doctor got up and quickly threw on some clothes and put her hair up, not sure what to expect. The doctor was expecting the worst when she arrived. After a twenty-minute carriage ride, she arrived at the Capulet castle. There she was met outside by Scott.

CHAPTER FIFTY-FOUR

BACK IN SERENITY'S bedroom, Yasha II walked in to check on Serenity while Scott waited for the doctor and General Charles was heading to her room to remove the enemy.

"Serenity, what's wrong? We heard you screaming from down the hall," asked Yasha II.

"I'm fine, just not feeling all that good," said Serenity, not knowing she was a shape-shifter and very sensitive to things.

After some time had passed, her brother Scott walked in with the doctor behind him.

"Sister, I got your doctor here, please let her take a look at you," pleaded Scott.

"Fine, brother, I'll let her take a look at me," said Serenity.

She only agreed since she was in so much pain to argue with her brother. Yasha II, who was standing next to her bed, stepped back, giving the doctor room. Reluctantly Serenity allowed Yasha II to step away from her.

"Prince Scott, please have everyone leave the room. I'll have to ask your sister some questions. She may be uncomfortable to answer in front of others," said the doctor.

"Okay, I'll be in my room and have others put into guest rooms," said Scott.

"Thank you, Prince Scott," said the doctor.

"Cloud, Fang, Yasha II, and Exotic, let's go. We will leave my sister in care of her doctor," said Scott.

"Fine, since that's what the doctor wants," said Fang and Yasha II, worried about what's going on with Serenity. Yasha II has a pretty good idea what was the cause of it or what was happening to Serenity, but he was keeping quiet about it. He knew everything would fall apart if the truth was known right now.

Serenity was trying to stay out of her oracle form, which was causing her pain resisting the form.

"Princess Serenity, the questions I'm going to ask you, I need you to answer me honestly," said the doctor.

"Okay, I'll try to answer them as honestly as I can," said Serenity.

"Good girl. When was the last time you had sex?" asked the doctor.

"Almost three months ago, and I haven't had my period yet," admitted Serenity.

The doctor got out her portable ultrasound machine to double-check see if she was pregnant and to clarify it.

"Please, not one of those again," said Serenity in a panic.

"Sorry, Princess Serenity, but I need to make sure nothing's wrong with you and to confirm what's going on," said the doctor.

The doctor put the gel on Serenity's stomach then put the hand scanner on the gel and started moving it around to check for anything out of normal and noticed that Serenity was with children. When Serenity looked at the tiny screen, she was in shock with the proof in front of her.

"Serenity, you need to stop trying suppressing the form you got pregnant in and go back into the form. It would be healthier for you," said the doctor.

"Doctor, can I still travel overseas?" asked Serenity.

"Yes, but you should take someone with you," said the doctor.

"Okay, I'll take Cloud, it won't raise any suspicion," said Serenity.

Serenity couldn't tell her father what happened between Yasha II and her back in Japan, at the Hathaway lands. Out of nowhere, due to Serenity's shocked reaction, Yasha II showed up in her room.

"Serenity, there's no way I'm letting you go this alone. It's my fault you're pregnant," said Yasha II.

"Yasha II, I was hoping you wouldn't come since the risk of being near my parents after I find them in China," said Serenity.

"What about your safety around your parents and on your journey?" said Yasha II.

"Fine, if it will put you at ease, then come, and my parents will have to get over it," said Serenity.

CHAPTER FIFTY-FIVE

SCOTT TOOK EXOTIC to his room knowing they both needed rest. Scott set Exotic up on his bed. He made sure the servants came in and put on clean bedding. He also had them bring in a mattress with a clean set of bedding on the floor for himself. He didn't want to move too fast with Exotic knowing he was in love with her. Exotic even can tell Scott has fallen in love with her. They both went to bed. Scott was on the floor bed, and Exotic was in his bed. Scott woke up in the middle of the night having to use the restroom; after using and walking back into room, he lay in his bed next to Exotic half asleep still.

A few hours before dawn, Exotic woke up. She noticed that somehow during the night, Scott ended up in the same bed as her. She was relieved that they were at least dressed. She went to get up to get fresh air, when Scott wrapped his arms around her in his sleep.

"Scott, please let me go, I need some fresh air," said Exotic.

"Okay, Exotic," said Scott.

Scott then let her up and got up himself as well. They both walked out onto the balcony to get some fresh air. Scott grabbed Exotic's hand and just held it while they stood on the balcony.

"Scott, does your sister like going outside during the daytime?" asked Exotic.

"No, due to her sensitive skin, as children, she always hides when I tried to get her to go outside during daytime," said Scott.

Scott thought back to the past when he was just a child and tried to get Serenity to play outside during the daytime with him. Scott was five, and Serenity just turned six. The very first time he tried to get her to go outside, she went with him not fully understanding how sensitive her skin was to the daylight. But it didn't last long; as soon as they got outside on a hot summer day to play, Serenity ran and hid among the trees where it was dark until nightfall. Scott always harassed his sister go outside and paly, but every time she got too close to a lot of sun, she ran and hid until she got old enough to understand that by covering her skin, she could go out for a while during the day without pain from being sensitive to light. As a child, he never understood why she wouldn't play outside with him. As children, she always was just getting up as he was going to bed most of the time. As children, he never understood why she always had more energy at night than he did. He never understood why she always had more energy at night than during the day, and he always had more energy during the day and not at night, compared to his sister. He never understood how different they were as children. He also remembers how hard their father was on Serenity when they were children. Even knowing their father was a vampire, he was always hard on Serenity when she was a child and wasn't resting during daytime hours.

When they were teenagers, he remembers always finding bruises on his sister the next morning and not understanding what was causing it. He remembers always seeing their older brother Jonathan around her until he turned eighteen and went into the army when they were ten. It was within a year of that that he started seeing the bruise on his sister and not trying to figure out what was hurting her. No matter what happened to Serenity during the night, he never heard her cry out for help. One of the worst nights in the castle he can recall was when they were teenagers, and Serenity's bloodcurdling screams and crying in pain were so loud that it woke him up out of a restful night's sleep one summer night.

Scott started rushing through the castle alarmed by his sister's screaming and crying out. When he was able to find his sister, she was all cut up by a weapon taken to her back, and the clothing she had on her back was torn to shreds. He looked to see who harmed his sister and was horrified to find out it was their father. Scott noticed that Serenity was unable to stand, shaking. The one person he knew who wasn't afraid of anything was afraid of their father.

The sight of his father standing there holding a bloody whip with blood dripping from it made Scott furious with rage. Their father, not even caring who witnessed it, went to bring down the whip on Serenity again, who was unable to stand and defend herself due to the blood loss.

Scott rushed toward his father trying to stop him from abusing his sister any further, ready to fight him and defend her. Their father surprised him by willing to do the same to his own son if he chose to get in the way. When Serenity looked up, she saw their father willing to go and whip Scott as well.

"No, brother! He will do the same to you as well," said Serenity.

"It's okay, sister, he won't touch you again," said Scott.

Serenity started crying, unable to stop her brother, and passed out from the blood loss.

Scott was pulled back to reality once Serenity's screams pierced the castle once again. He noticed Exotic fell back to sleep as they were standing outside. He carried her back to bed and covered her up before quietly leaving the room to go check on Serenity in a panic. He worried that someone had hurt her again and was why she screamed. After he rushed to his sister's room and opened her door, he found her thrashing around in her sleep. He scanned the room to see if Yasha II was still with her. He noticed Yasha II was missing and drag marks that led out of the room, as if a struggle happened. Scott went over to wake his sister up to make sure she was all right before going to find General Charles and find out what happened to Yasha II.

Back in Scott's room, Exotic woke up to find that Scott was missing and she was no longer out on the balcony. Exotic decided to get dressed and go find Scott, not sure what was going on. She was not sure how much she could explore without an escort and not get into trouble for it. She searched for him; she found herself in a wing far away from where she was. She sensed he been inside room that behind door. She was hoping whoever was in there could give her answers, so before she thought it through, she opened the door. She found a woman behind it who was a bit older than Scott and herself. The woman has long silver hair, silver eyes, pale skin, and black falcon wings coming from her back. She also found Scott with her. Scott's attention went from his sister to Exotic, who just entered the room.

"Exotic, what are you doing here?" asked Scott, not sure how to explain why he was in his sister's room.

"I was worried something was wrong when I woke up and you weren't there," said Exotic calmly, not sure what to make of what she was seeing.

"I was pulled out of my thoughts while we dozed off on the balcony due to my sister screaming," said Scott.

"Okay, is there anything I can do to help?" asked Exotic.

"If you wouldn't mind keeping my sister company? I need to go talk to General Charles," said Scott.

"Okay, I can do that for you," said Exotic.

Scott walked out of Serenity's room panicked, hoping Charles didn't have something do with Yasha II's disappearance from Serenity's room.

Exotic approached Serenity with caution. Serenity felt Exotic's aura of nervousness and flared up defensively. It caused a fire to surround Serenity that is harmless unless you try to touch her than one that gets to close without her wanting them to will get burned. Cloud barged in the room sensing Serenity's emotions and magic all flurried up.

"Princess Exotic, calm down, or please back away from Serenity. She is reacting to your aura," said Cloud.

"Who the fuck are you telling me what to do!" demanded Exotic, and her aura flurried up with rage and making Serenity's magic worse.

"I don't have time to argue with you. The angrier and more upset you get, the more Serenity reacts, and she's unpredictable right now," said Cloud.

"Fine, I was just trying help," said Exotic.

Exotic left the room, pissed off at Cloud's behavior. She decided to head back to Scott's room, not having to put up with Cloud. Cloud rushed over to Serenity and put his wings around her to calm her down. Serenity started to relax at the soft touch of Cloud's wings around her.

CHAPTER FIFTY-SIX

SCOTT FINALLY FOUND General Charles after finding the general's office. Scott barged into the office and walked up to General Charles sitting at his desk doing paper. He looked up to see Scott standing in front of him.

"Prince Scott, can I help you?" asked General Charles.

"Yes, where is Yasha II? My sister is upset since his sudden disappearance," said Scott.

"Why do you think I had anything to do with that?" asked General Charles.

"Charles, don't play stupid with me. I may not be the lord here, but I am your prince. I also know that Yasha II is our family enemy, also the enemy of your princess," said Scott.

"Fine, if you want the truth, I forced Yasha II to leave the lands," said General Charles.

"How did you do that?" demanded Scott, having a pretty good idea that it has do with Yasha II being an enemy of the royal family.

"I gave him the option of leaving the lands or being thrown in the dungeon," said General Charles.

"Charles, I had it with you. This time you've gone too far forcing Yasha II to leave. I will punish you myself, so that way, my sister doesn't have to worry about finding an appropriate punishment for your actions," said Scott.

Scott knew he couldn't remove him as Serenity's royal guard and general of the guards that protected her. So he knew he needs to settle on a job that Charles hated doing.

"Charles, you need to do the servants' job for week on top of your normal duties," ordered Scott.

Charles looked at Scott pissed off about his punishment. Charles absolutely hated doing servant's work.

"Fine, Prince Scott, as you command," said Charles.

Scott left Charles to seek out Serenity's doctor and speak with her.

***

In China, Janine and Jonathan have secured a home and a job to make sure they could maintain appearances of a commoner. Janine, being a devoted wife and learned the skills at a young age, did all work around their house they have in China, on top of the job she has, even though she was a royal. China was an easier place for Janine and Jonathan to hide in than their home country or America; they have fewer vampire hunters. But it was still a matter of time before they were discovered.

One evening, a group of VHs came into the casino that Janine and Jonathan worked at. Janine hasn't let her guard down since they came to China, knowing hunters could attack them on a moment's notice. When they walked into the casino, Janine spotted the hunters right off. Janine went to her husband's side attentively. But she did it in a timely fashion not to draw attention of the hunters to herself.

"Jonathan baby, we need to leave now," said Janine in a calm tone.

Jonathan made Janine join him as they left their temporary jobs, not to return. They knew that now they needed to secure new place to work and find a new home. They headed back to their home to collect what they had before relocating to a different part of China. They would need to find new jobs and lodgings when they finally find another area. They headed to the airport and changed passports to escape the VHs. They booked the next flight out of China, and that flight was heading to Iceland. Janine was hoping that Serenity would be able to figure out that they changed locations since they were compromised. But they also knew it unwise to suddenly return back home, not sure what was going on with the lands or how many hunters were looking for them in Russia.

CHAPTER FIFTY-SEVEN

SCOTT FOUND THE doctor's room easily and knocked on the door.

"Come in," said the doctor.

Scott opened the door and walked in hoping to hear some good news about his sister's condition.

"How can I help you, Prince Scott?" asked Dr. Julia.

"Can my sister keep traveling, or should she stop?" asked Prince Scott.

"It wouldn't be in her best interest to keep traveling, but that's only something she can decide," said Dr. Julia.

"But what if I couldn't stop her from traveling?" asked Prince Scott.

"Then don't let her ride her horse alone, and make sure she doesn't push herself too far," said Julia.

"Okay, I'll make sure it happens, then I'll horse back with her or someone who's close to her," said Prince Scott.

Scott left Dr. Julia's office and walked back across the castle and went to Serenity's room and knocked on the door. He knew that he needed talk with his sister before leaving to meet up with her companions and head back to Captain Mason's ship to go after their parents that were waiting for them in China, last they knew. Scott had to know what his sister had gotten herself into, but only she can explain it to him clearly since her doctor wouldn't tell him anything about her.

"The door is open, come on in," said Serenity.

Serenity was sitting on the edge of her bed dressed and ready to head out again to try and find her parents. Even though she knew they weren't her birth parents, she still needed the truth.

"Sister, what happened with you while we were in Japan?" asked Scott.

"Sorry, brother, I'm keeping most of that a secret," said Serenity.

She worried that if her brother Scott knew too much, then he would tell Jonathan, her adoptive father. She knew he'd do something bad to her or her mate, so she didn't tell him anything. She knew she won't be able to hide the truth forever, but she was determined to for as long as she can.

"Brother, can we please leave and head to the port and go after our parents? I would like to make sure we can head to China on Captain Mason's ship," asked Serenity.

"All right, I'll have them prepare the horse for the ride to the port right away," said Scott.

"Thank you, brother," said Serenity.

Scott went back to his room to get Exotic and pack enough clothes for a week's trip, knowing they could have laundry done for them on the ship. They all met in the barn to get the horses to leave. A horse-drawn carriage was also prepared, but that mainly was just carrying their luggage. Serenity went to get on Icicle to ride to the port, but both Scott and Cloud stopped her.

"Serenity, you should ride with your brother Scott or me," said Cloud.

"But, Cloud, I want to ride Icicle," said Serenity.

"I will allow it only if you allow me to ride on her with you," said Cloud.

"Fine, Cloud," said Serenity, not wanting to argue over it.

Serenity, Scott, Exotic, Cloud, and Sasha all left the Capulet stables in silence. When they were finally outside the Capulet lands, they were met by Fang and Yasha II. Cloud was surprised to see Fang. Serenity was the only one able to see Yasha II in front of them as well.

"Where were you, Fang? Hiding? I couldn't pick up your presence from the castle or when we got outside the Capulet lands," asked Cloud.

"Magic to conceal our presence," said Fang.

"Fang, where is Yasha II? He hasn't been around since I found him with Serenity in the castle," asked Cloud.

"I'm not sure," said Fang, unable to see Yasha II as well.

"Fang, do you want to be the one riding with Serenity?" asked Cloud.

"Wouldn't it be pointless with you already on the horse with her?" asked Fang.

"You may have a point with that," said Cloud.

Serenity noticed Yasha II but didn't dare say anything or even look in his direction. She didn't dare ask to have Yasha II ride with her to keep the secret that he was the one she wanted. She couldn't let on that Prince Yasha II was the father. Serenity couldn't have them knowing she was an oracle as well. She was not even sure she was a normal shapeshifter with the ability of an oracle. This secret must be guarded until she knew the full truth. Serenity started playing with the necklace that Yasha II gave her with his family crest on it. Scott noticed the necklace that his sister was playing with.

"Cloud, whose necklace and family crest is it that my sister is clinging to and playing with nervously?" asked Scott.

"I believe it belongs to a man named Yasha Vasiliev II," said Cloud.

"You allowed him alone with her?" demanded Scott.

"We had no choice. We got separated from her when she took off into the ruins. Before we knew what was going on, a small gap in time was frozen at Lord Hathaway's castle."

"Oh, great, my father may try to kill both you and Yasha II for this," said Scott.

"Let him try to kill my kind or an archangel," said Cloud.

Scott shut up, forgetting who he was dealing with and what Cloud and Yasha II were. Scott hasn't personally met Yasha II, but he knew if Cloud was speaking the truth, it would be a mistake to underestimate Yasha II.

After an hour of travelling, Cloud, Fang, and Yasha II made it to the port. Scott, Sasha, and Exotic still hadn't made it to the port yet. Serenity, Yasha II, Fang, and Cloud got on the ship first. Captain Mason walked up to Yasha II and Serenity.

"Yasha II, is everything all right with Serenity?" asked Captain Mason.

"She is healthy, nothing is wrong with her," said Yasha II.

"But she was getting sick last time she was on my ship, and that is not normal for her," said Captain Mason.

"Captain Mason, I was cleared to travel, and right now, I couldn't explain what's going. I just need you to trust me," said Serenity.

"Okay, Princess Serenity," said Captain Mason.

"Captain Mason, could I ask a favor from you?" asked Serenity.

"Sure, anything for you, Princess Serenity," said Captain Mason.

"Can you please grant Yasha II and Fang protection from my family guards until we leave Russia?" asked Serenity.

"Yes, my princess," said Captain Mason.

Serenity, Yasha II, and Fang all got aboard the ship. Serenity went to Captain Mason's private quarters with Yasha II and Fang following her. Serenity lay down on Captain Mason's bed hoping everyone would be safe from her family guards. Yasha II lay down next to her in hopes of comforting her.

"Yasha II, please don't leave me alone again," asked Serenity.

"I won't if I can help it, but as long as you're near or with the Capulet family, I may be forced to leave or at least appear to be invisible and not here at times," said Yasha II, frowning.

Serenity was about to start crying. When all a sudden, Yasha II wrapped his arms and wings around her. He wanted to keep her calm and safe even if it won't always be easy.

"Calm down, Princess Serenity, I'll always be watching over you and nearby. Even if you can't see me, I'd be in a safe distance," said Yasha II.

"Is that a promise?" asked Serenity with half a smile.

"Yes, one I will keep forever if you believe in me and in us," said Yasha II.

Serenity fell asleep in Yasha II's arms. Yasha II made sure his wings were wrapped around her and himself to keep her safe. He joined her in sleep. A few hours later, there was pounding at the door. Then the next thing he heard was Scott's voice from the other side of the door.

"Yasha II, open the door. I was followed by my family royal guard to the ship," demanded Scott.

"Why should I, so they can arrest me and hurt Princess Serenity in the process? I don't think so," yelled Yasha II, protective of Serenity's heart and emotions.

Captain Mason went to check on Serenity and spotted Charles and Scott on his ship near his private quarters.

"General Charles, if you are looking to arrest Yasha II or Fang, get the hell off my ship," ordered Captain Mason.

"Watch your tongue, captain, you are on Russian soil," warned General Charles.

"No, this is my homeland, and I go by what Princess Serenity wants, not what her parents want," said Captain Mason.

Charles took out his sword, pissed off at Captain Mason's insolence and ready to kill him for it. Serenity took two steps with her magic and ended up between Captain Mason and General Charles.

"GENERAL CHARLES GRINCORY, GO THE HELL HOME, YOU HAVE NO AUTHORITY HERE!" yelled Serenity.

Right after yelling at her head general, she collapsed, falling backward into Captain Mason's arms. The port officer rushed on the ship hearing yelling and found that Captain Mason caught a young woman in his arms.

"Captain Mason, are you having any trouble?" asked the port patrol officer.

"Yes, please remove this man," asked Captain Mason, pointing at General Charles.

"Sir, we need to ask you to kindly leave, or we can remove you by force from the ship," said the port patrol officer.

"Fine, I'll leave since I don't need any trouble," said General Charles.

He walked off the ship of his own accord and started walking back to the Capulet lands, knowing that her father would deal with her rebellion. He wished Princess Serenity was calling on him, not some prince that her family enemy. He felt anger growing inside of him and getting angrier at himself for being jealous of the enemy and letting his nature get the better of him.

CHAPTER FIFTY-EIGHT

NIKOLAI BELIKOV, A spirit, entered Serenity's dream. Serenity came face-to-face with him not recognizing him at first.

"Who are you, and why do you look so much like me?" asked Serenity, surprised to see someone like her.

The main difference between her and him was that he was a male, not female like her, so she wanted to know what about him made her think she was so much like him and never met him before. As far as she can recall, she'd only been around Janine and Jonathan.

"Yes, I do, sweetheart. You will be in grave danger if you go after Janine and Jonathan. Jonathan will kill both Fang and Yasha II if he sees them," warned the spirit of Nikolai Belikov.

"Who are you, and how do you know all this?" asked Serenity.

"I'll explain in time, but I need you to take care of yourself," said the spirit of Nikolai Belikov.

Serenity woke up Yasha II, screaming her name.

"I'm okay, I promise, Yasha II," said Serenity before realizing she was crying for no reason.

"Then why are you crying?" asked Yasha II.

"It's just a dream I had," said Serenity.

"Can you please tell me about the dream?" asked Yasha.

"Let me get more rest first, then I'll tell," said Serenity.

"Okay, but take your seasickness pill first so it has time to kick in before we set sail and leave port," said Yasha II.

"Okay," said Serenity, taking it to appease him and to allow herself to rest.

Nikolai appeared in Serenity's dream once more. He wanted to find a way to help his daughter even though she didn't fully understand what was going on.

"Sweetheart, you need to take it easy. Let me show you the past and possible future," said the spirit of Nikolai Belikov.

His voice sent Serenity into a relaxed state. She was brought to another world or life before she was born. She saw before her, her actual birth mother.

"Nikolai love, please come to bed," asked Irshrose.

"Okay, love," said Nikolai.

Her mother looked about eighteen years old and like she was pregnant and about to give birth. Nikolai walked into their bedroom to find his wife breathing heavy and unevenly. Nikolai called for his wife's physician.

"My lord, how can I help you?" asked Dr. Julia.

"I need you to tend to my wife. She's starting to breath heavy and unevenly," said Lord Belikov.

"My lord, there is little I can do for her," said Dr. Julia.

"What do you mean you couldn't do much for my wife?" demanded Lord Belikov.

"Calm down, my lord, it only simple means that your wife has gone into labor," said Dr. Julia.

"But we've only done it once since when we were in high school. We were sixteen on a summer vacation while we were alone," said Lord Belikov.

"That's all it takes, but it takes about two years for any children you will have to develop," said Dr. Julia.

While Lord Belikov and Dr. Julia were talking in the hallway, they heard screaming coming from inside the room. Dr. Julia rushed inside to check on Irshrose and found she was about to have the baby and needed assistance. Julia was able help Irshrose deliver a healthy baby boy. Julia cleaned up the baby boy and handed him to his father before double-checking on Irshrose. When she went to check on Irshrose, her patient, she noticed her missing. But Irshrose shouldn't have been able to without eating food first.

"My lord, we had a security breach," said his general.

"Find my wife now, General Ace, that's an order," demanded Lord Belikov.

"Julia, take the young prince somewhere safe. I will have you return him when it is safe or when he turns eighteen so he can watch over these lands until the princess and rightful heir is born and returns here," said Lord Belikov.

He had a decree made that no son of his will become ruler but will become protectors of the princess.

Nikolai then took her to another scene from the past; it was twelve years later. He was face-to-face with Lord Jonathan Capulet. She watched as the scene played out. Lord Capulet and Lord Belikov were fighting to the death. Lord Capulet took a cheap shot and threw Lord Belikov off-balance. Irshrose tried to get free to help Nikolai. Nikolai tried to counterattack but failed due to the fact he was partly blind. But he had his way of knowing people. He used his sixth sense to fight and show affection toward others. Irshrose screamed as Nikolai collapsed to the ground, clinging on to life, wanting to live. Jonathan claimed Irshrose and her four-year-old daughter, leaving Nikolai for dead.

Serenity was then taken from the past and into the future. She was in a land that she only heard about in myths. It looked like everything was made of crystal and ice. She was taken through the lands and into the castle next; it was breathtaking—made from crystals of all colors. The castle stood twenty stories tall. Its shape was unique. The castle was made more out of round towers with peaks on the top; they were connected by walls that you can walk through because the middle of the walls were hollow, and you could walk on top of the walls, and every wall had a gate in the middle of each wall. In the middle of all the towers and inside walls and in between all the towers was a garden. There were four medium-size towers on corner, and the middle of two in the back was a large tower where the royal family lived, and it had a ballroom, library, kitchen, throne room, and royal chambers in four hallways. The royal tomb was also in the main part of the castle. She was shown the whole castle in the vision. She was shown four rooms fitting of a prince/princess. She wanted to know whose rooms they were before and why so much in the room have been untouched. She was guessing it's been almost twenty-six years since anything had been touched in these rooms. The large tower was a hundred feet wide and fifty stories high.

"I'll tell you why, sweetheart. I was killed, and your mother was unable to return here," said Nikolai.

"I want to go there," said Serenity out loud.

"One day you will, but we need to help your mother first," said Nikolai.

Serenity frowned knowing she had to help her mother first before going to her father's lands.

CHAPTER FIFTY-NINE

SERENITY WOKE UP to the sound of engines starting. She looked up at Yasha II.

"Love, you be okay, we're just getting ready to leave the port and set sail to China. By the way, Captain Mason stopped in to check on you. I told him you will be fine," said Yasha.

"Yasha II, do you think the doctor will be back?" asked Serenity.

"Yes, to make sure everything is all right with you," said Yasha II.

Serenity went back to sleep since it was still daytime, plus she was tired. The return home, then leaving right away again was taking a toll on her body, specially under these circumstances. Serenity was happy as long as she has Yasha II at her side. If he was here, nothing else really mattered to her.

In Serenity's dreams, she was once again being shown visions of the past, but this time even more recent. She was being shown China about two hours ago; the place where Janine and Jonathan were hiding. She saw her adoptive mother doing her job until vampire hunters came barging in the casino. Janine ran to Jonathan.

"Jonathan, you must leave, vampire hunters have shown up here," said Janine.

Jonathan grabbed her so that she had to leave with him.

Serenity was once again shown a vision of a crystal and ice castle once again. This time three princes were gathered around two figures swearing their loyalty to them. The figures became clear as the princes stepped aside and bowed as figures walked past them. The woman was her, but she was wondering why she looked young still. What she didn't know about her bloodline was they don't age after a certain age. She was not sure why she felt she can trust this spirit whom she did not know as her father while growing up. All these questions were running through her head.

"I could answer all these questions for you, sweetheart," said Nikolai.

"Okay, then please help me understand more about what I'm supposed to be doing," said Serenity.

Nikolai took Serenity in his arms and held her in her dream. But she could still feel the hug physically, as if the dream came to life. "It's still a dream," she had to tell herself. Serenity felt a rush of calming breeze over her. A safety and protection spell went around her. A normal demon or human wouldn't be able to see a spirit. She was anything but ordinary.

CHAPTER SIXTY

IT WAS 1:00 a.m. in Iceland when Jonathan and Janine settled into a hotel room that was attached to a casino that they would be working at. Their new boss supplied them with a room that they could use all along as they needed it while working for him. Jonathan went work right away for four hours. Janine decided to go to bed, not having to work until noon. Janine was relieved to finally have a little time to herself for the first time in a while.

Janine's mind started to wonder about Serenity. She was wondering about her beautiful adopted daughter. She wanted to know what she was doing right now, if she found any allies to count on or if she found one of Jonathan's enemies. It would be granted if she ran into Yasha II or Fang again, a childhood friend of Serenity. She knew how much Serenity liked to disobey the rules and authority of others. Janine knew how dangerous both Yasha II and Fang were and what they were. There was no doubt in her mind that if Jonathan became a threat to Serenity, then Yasha II and Fang would stop at nothing to kill Jonathan. Hell, she knew Serenity would do it herself if pushed over the edge. Janine wanted to call Serenity but knew it was not part of the plan. So she just went to sleep with an uneasy feeling that her adopted daughter was heading to a danger zone. China became home to VHS, and they were still looking for them.

Serenity was just waking up after sleeping most of the day. It was 6:00 p.m. and time for dinner, so Serenity got up to go have dinner with the rest of the passengers. Yasha II woke up to her movement.

"Serenity, are you all right?" asked Yasha II.

"Yes, I just need some food. I'm hungry and need to move I'm sorry for waking you up," said Serenity.

"It's okay, Serenity, I'm just being overprotective and fell asleep with my wings wrapped around you," said Yasha II.

"Yasha, don't be so hard on yourself," said Serenity smiling, liking that he was being protective of her.

Serenity got up a and walked across the room. She left Yasha II inside while she went and got some dinner. In the dining room, she was meet by everyone else. Scott, her younger brother, looked at her shocked that she looked so healthy and was up walking around. Captain Mason walked into the dining hall to get some dinner. He walked over to Serenity after spotting her and seeing her healthy.

"Excuse me, Princess Serenity," said Captain Mason.

"Can I help you, Captain Mason?" asked Princess Serenity.

"Princess, please join me for dinner," asked Captain Mason.

Scott went from shocked about Serenity being healthy to mortified in less than ten seconds in being in the same room as his sister. Serenity felt her brother Scott's emotion from across the room.

"Captain Mason, what about my brother? He's gotten the wrong idea about your relationship with me," asked Princess Serenity.

"Would you like me to explain it to him, or do you prefer to do it yourself, my princess?" asked Captain Mason.

"I will do it. He'll be more likely to understand it and listen if it's coming from me," said Princess Serenity.

Serenity decided to join Captain Mason for dinner and explain it all to Scott later, even though she could feel vibes from her brother Scott. Mason was a friend to her; it didn't matter how many years it's been since she last saw him. She and Captain Mason went to the captain's table as Fang and Yasha walked into the room and saw Scott's mortified look and started laughing. Shortly after, Cloud, Sasha, and Exotic entered the dining hall and joined in laughing at Scott's expression.

Serenity was unsure what to do knowing why they were laughing. Scott got up and left mortified with this whole situation. Serenity went to get up and leave to go after Scott and explain but knew it would be best to allow him to blow off some steam before even attempting to tell him the truth. Serenity remained seated so she could get herself something to eat after resting up most of the day. Serenity felt a chilling but relaxing breeze flow over her. She started to wonder if it was possible for a spirit to make its presence known in a room. Serenity knew in the back of her mind that she would give anything to see who her biological father was.

CHAPTER SIXTY-ONE

ROZA WAS CLEANING Princess Serenity's room, so it won't be dusty when she returned home. Roza knew how much Serenity hated her room to be dusty. She started to reflect on the past. Serenity always tried to do the maid's job when they got a day off. She liked to keep her room clean and organized. Rosa, however, understood why since she grew up in a worse part of the castle. Where Roza slept, it was never cleaned or dusted daily. All the adult maids and servants were too lazy to keep their living area clean. Rosa knew her mother was the exception. She was always too embarrassed to tell Serenity where she stayed. If she could tell Serenity now, she would be proud to show Serenity where she slept.

It had changed since she's been made head of the maids and servants. It's only been a few months since being the active head of the maids and servants, but she intended to keep the authority over the other maids and servants after Lord Capulet returns and appoints an actual head of the maids and servants. Roza was pulled from the past and her thoughts when another maid addressed her.

"Roza, why are you in Princess Serenity's room?" asked another maid.

"It must stay clean even when she is away," said Roza.

"Oh, does the princess hate a messy and dusty room?" asked the other maid.

"Yes, growing up with her, she tried cleaning her room when the maids had a day off, when they didn't have to do her room," said Roza.

The maid left the room mad; they don't get a break cleaning the princess's room. Roza went back to her job. She was bothered by the fact that Serenity didn't allow herself anytime to rest before traveling after her parents.

***

Cloud, Sasha, Fang, and Yasha II were on the bow of the ship. They were all to address one of the major issues with this trip.

"Yasha II and Fang, are you sure you both want to be with us when we see Janine and Jonathan?" asked Cloud.

"Yes, her father doesn't scare me. I'm more afraid what he will do to Serenity when he finds out the truth of what's going on," said Yasha II.

"Let Jonathan try to harm. He will get what's coming to him. I'll protect Serenity from him if he tries to harm her," said Fang.

"What truth is it that you're so concerned about?" asked Cloud. He asked even though he was pretty sure he already knew the answer.

"The fact that she is pregnant by the enemy and is in love with that person," said Yasha II, knowing he was referring to himself.

"Well, you're in trouble now, Yasha II," said Cloud, knowing Yasha II was referring to himself.

"Shut the hell up, will you, Cloud?" said Yasha II, angry with Cloud.

Cloud started laughing uncontrollably at Yasha's anger toward him and fell to the ground laughing before he realized how hard he was laughing at Yasha II. Sasha stared at Cloud then at Yasha.

"Yasha, it will be best if you leave this to Cloud and I after we reach Iceland," said Sasha.

"Why should I? Serenity is my girlfriend and my responsibility," said Yasha.

"You may be her boyfriend, but what good are you going to be to her in jail?" said Sasha.

"You have a point. I'll back off some and let you guys help. But I swear if Scott says anything to his parents, he will have his ass kicked," said Yasha.

Yasha didn't trust Scott. Sasha nodded in agreement with Yasha. When Cloud rejoined the conversation, Sasha and Yasha were done talking.

"Sasha and Yasha, what where you decision," asked Cloud.

"I'm not repeating myself because of your lack of self-control," said Sasha bitterly with a Japanese accent.

She could speak both English and Russian fluently. Cloud decided to walk away knowing he pissed off Sasha. Yasha decided to return to his room hoping he would find Serenity there resting some more. Fang returned to his room sad, disappointed, knowing he didn't find Serenity there waiting for her. Yasha found an envelope on his nightstand. It had his name on and Serenity's royal seal on the back of it. He opened it, and this is what he read:

> Dear Yasha,
> I need to think something through and talk to my brother. I need to straighten him out on few subjects. If I'm not back by 2 a.m. come look for me. If you do make sure you aren't carrying any fire power or leave most of it behind. I don't want no one injured that is an innocent bystander, please I don't want any unnecessary trouble onboard Captain Mason's ship.
>
> I love you,
> Serenity Irshrose Capulet

Serenity has been in Scott's room for an hour in absolute silence. Serenity broke the silence between them.

"Brother, I believe you are reading into some of my relationships the wrong way," said Serenity.

"Serenity, how is it that you aren't sleeping with Captain Mason?" asked Scott.

"Scott, I'm not in love with Captain Mason, and I have never slept with him. Yasha is my only love," said Serenity, ticking off Scott.

She got up and left slamming the door behind her. She left Scott pissed off and headed back to see Yasha needing to calm down and relax. After a few minutes, she was grabbed from behind by two unknow assailants. They knocked her out before she had the chance to scream for help. Serenity was still able to send a telepathic signal to Yasha and Cloud that she was in trouble again. Cloud, Yasha, Fang, and Sasha all split up to see if she was still on the ship. Even though there was a slim chance that she was no longer on the ship at all.

"Sasha, please go take watch outside of Scott's room, and make sure they won't come back for him. We will go after the princess," said Cloud.

"Yes, Cloud, I understand," said Sasha.

CHAPTER SIXTY-TWO

SERENITY WOKE TO find herself yet again in another VHS base. This one was far different from the last one she was in. She heard noises outside the room she was in. She looked out the tinted window and could tell they were in a downtown area; she was just not sure what country yet. Serenity looked closely at the signs, and they were not Russian, so she studied the signs closer and identified them as Chinese. A land that she somehow was very familiar with. If she could escape and make it to the capital, she could take refuge among the army. But that was if she could convince them to take a female into their ranks.

She knew how risky this whole mission of hers was. She decided to take her bare hands and break the window. Her hand bled only as long as it took her to take out the glass in it. She jumped out the window and onto the roof of the building across from the one she was being held in. She was lucky that the VHs didn't know how quickly she heals. Once they entered the room from hearing the breaking glass, they noticed her gone and blood on the floor. Serenity was running across and jumping from rooftop to rooftop to escape the VHs that were chasing her. Serenity made it out of town and was running through the woods toward the capital. Once she reached the capital, she got as close as possible to the palace. The major problem would be trying get their protection from the VHS. When she got close to the palace, an army camp was guarding it. The two guards at the gate approached her.

"Miss, no civilians are allowed beyond these walls," said one of the two guards of the gate.

"Please, I need protection from vampire hunters," said Serenity.

"Sorry, we don't accept your kind among our ranks," said the other guard.

The general walked over noticing the guards were out of place and a young female that appeared to be a vampire standing in front of the gate.

"Men, what seems to be the problem?" asked General Jacob.

"She claims vampire hunters are after her and won't leave the premise," said one guard.

"Miss, follow me. I want to have a word with you in private," said General Jacob.

"Yes, sir," said Serenity before following him away from the guards at the gate.

They walked about five minutes before entering a large general tent. The tent was big enough to hold a group of thirty or more inside.

"Now that we are alone, I have a few questions for you," said General Jacob.

"I will answer them as best as I can," said Serenity.

All of a sudden, after finally being caught up to her story, she realized she hadn't eaten or rested in she doesn't know how long since the VHS took her; she yawned, and her stomach started to growl. She was tired and hungry.

"Miss, are you okay?" asked General Jacob, concerned about her health.

"Yes, I just haven't had anything to eat or have much rest," said Serenity.

General Jacob decided to take her to rest before giving her food and questioning her father. They walked to his tent, which was close to by, and she lay down on the bed. Serenity fell asleep right away, exhausted from running away from the vampire hunters again. She slipped into her natural form, which looked similar to a vampire but her wings were showing. General Jacob headed back to work and planned to check on her later.

It's around noontime when a group of hunters approached the army camp outside the capital. General Jacob was making his rounds when he spotted a suspicious group of men near the camp.

"Gentlemen, what brings you near the army camp for?" asked General Jacob.

"We are looking for this woman. Have you seen her?" asked the hunter, showing General Jacob a photo of Serenity.

"Sorry, but I haven't seen her," said General Jacob.

General Jacob lied to them since they didn't look friendly and suspected they didn't have good intentions toward her. The men left thinking she may have decided to hide elsewhere until nightfall. Jacob was relieved that they fell for his lie but was not sure if they would come back to try to find her.

CHAPTER SIXTY-THREE

IT TOOK YASHA, Fang, and Cloud half a day's flight, but they made it to China. They spotted a group of hunters right away and blocked their path.

"Men, can we get by, please? You are blocking the street," asked the head vampire hunter.

"No, not without answering a few questions first," said Yasha, pissed off.

"What does an archangel oracle want with us?" asked the head vampire hunter.

"Where is Serenity?" demanded Yasha.

"She ran away from us. We don't have her current location," said the head vampire hunter.

Yasha walked away and could tell they weren't lying to him. Cloud, on the other hand, punched the head vampire hunter for endangering her. Yasha was too focused on finding Serenity to punish the vampire hunters they ran into.

Yasha noticed an army camp and went to go inside and noticed the army men staring at him. General Jacob decided to approach the man walking toward them, knowing he shouldn't be within the army camp walls.

"Sir, I need to ask you to leave. Civilians aren't allowed in these walls," said General Jacob.

"Sorry, sir, you aren't making me leave without giving me Serenity first," said Yasha.

"Sorry, she is resting and not leaving here against her will," said General Jacob.

"Fine, we can wait until she wakes up and see what she wants," said Yasha.

"Okay, but I'm not letting you out of my sight," said General Jacob.

Yasha didn't dare disagree with him if he wanted to see Serenity again.

Serenity woke up and left the tent hungry for food. She spotted the guards from earlier that day while looking for the dining hall, when Yasha found her.

"Serenity, what are you up to?" asked Yasha.

"I'm trying find food. I'm hungry and need to speak with General Jacob," said Serenity.

The general walked up to her as she met up with Yasha.

"Serenity, what are you doing up and about?" asked General Jacob.

"I got hungry, and I'm looking for food." She was starting to get the urge to just feed off a member of the army just to calm fact she needs food.

Yasha grabbed her, sensing she was about to do something stupid, to prevent harm coming to anyone.

"Serenity, relax, calm down. We got you food. Don't forget you're carrying our child," said Yasha in a whisper to her.

Serenity calmed down, not wanting lose it or have Yasha in trouble for her losing it. Serenity started to go weak from not being able to hold herself up anymore, needing food. Yasha made sure that Serenity wouldn't fall to the ground from being weak. General Jacob went to get her some food to eat to restore her energy. Yasha put his wings around Serenity while they waited for General Jacob to return. He wanted to keep her protected in case she acted, before thinking it could be him who'd get bitten and not a member of the army.

CHAPTER SIXTY-FOUR

SCOTT, EXOTIC, AND Sasha were still two days away from China and still didn't know anything about Serenity's whereabouts. Sasha was staying close to Scott to protect him like Cloud. Everything he did, she was right behind him, except for the bathroom. Sasha planned to keep her word to Cloud. She felt like she could trust Cloud. Sasha found herself thinking about Cloud more and more. Exotic noticed Sasha staring into space, spacing out like a lovesick puppy. Exotic walked up to Sasha, concerned.

"Sasha, is something wrong? You look like a lovesick puppy," asked Exotic.

"Yes, I keep thinking about Cloud and don't know why," said Sasha.

"Well, it means you're in love and destined for each other," said Exotic.

"Maybe you're right. I've never been in love before," said Sasha, smiling.

After a while, they all went to bed. Scott and Exotic slept on his bed. Sasha slept in wolf form, lying on the floor, facing the door, ready to attack any intruder.

CHAPTER SIXTY-FIVE

JANINE WAS WOKEN up by her room phone going off the hook.

"Hello, this is Janine. How can I help you?" answered Janine.

"We need your assistance downstairs. We are busy and short-staffed. You are the only bouncer available," said the evening manager.

"Fine, I'll be right there after I get changed," said Janine and hung up the phone.

Janine jumped out of bed and went to get dressed for work. She pulled back her long red hair and up in a bun. Then she threw on her black top on; the right side says her name with the casino logo above it, and on the left, it says *bouncer* on it. The back gave the name of the casino. She also put on black jeans and black boots. She checked herself in the mirror to make sure she was presentable for work before leaving her room since she was the only one on call. The rest were either sick or already working.

When she got downstairs, she realized it was three times busier than normal. A bunch of tourists were all gambling and drinking. Janine would do anything to be security tonight; it was her favorite job, and she missed it a lot. Janine's night boss came over to her, which could mean many things.

"Janine, do you have any experience in the security department?" asked the night manager.

"Yes, I did it at my previous job," said Janine.

"Go met up with the head of security to get your new uniform and duty instructions," said the night manager.

"Yes, sir," said Janine.

She walked away happy getting into security. The head security guard stopped her. He was younger than her. He had black hair, brown eyes, and white skin. He was wearing black boots, black jeans, and a blue button-down shirt. On the back, it said *security* in gold print. On the front left and side of his shirt was his name under the logo, and the right said *head of security*. He was wearing an earpiece on his left ear, and a taser gun was attached to his side.

"Miss, are you the one being reassigned to us?" asked the head of security.

"Yes, I am," said Janine.

"Are you trained to use a taser and a gun?" asked the head of security.

Janine pulled out her licensee to carry a concealed weapon and handed it to the head of security as proof. Flame looked over the license, and when he was satisfied it wasn't a fake, he approved her for the position.

"My name is Flame. I am head of security, and you will only report to me or the manager on duty. I'm assigning to level two of the casino. Go get changed and report to your post," said the head of security.

"Yes, will do gladly," said Janine.

Janine wished she didn't have to quit when it came time to return home to Russia. But she was not going to concern herself with that for now. She had a job to do. Janine was glad she already memorized the layout of the casino in the short time they've been here. The one thing that still worried her was if Serenity was staying out of trouble. She wondered where Serenity was at right now and if she was going to end up in a fight when she found them. She had a feeling that she already found out that Nikolai Belikov is her father and Jonathan is not.

Johnathan just got off shift from bartending on the second floor and started walking back from the bar to his hotel room. All of a sudden, without paying attention, he slammed into his wife, Janine.

"Jonathan, watch where you are going, will you? No one needs to be run over by you," said Janine.

Jonathan jumped back, shocked at her voice being the one reminding him from almost running her over.

"Janine, why are you going in this late? I thought you had the night shift off," said Jonathan, surprised to see his wife.

"I did until I got called in and reassigned to security because they are shorthanded tonight," said Janine happily.

"Good for you. I'm going to grab a bite to eat and hit the sack," said Jonathan.

"Oh, okay, sounds like you had a busy night, my love," said Janine.

"Yes, more than I'm used to. Good night, love," said Jonathan.

Janine was having a lot of mixed feelings about a lot of things. She also hadn't seen her brother Jason Hathaway in a very long time and would like to see him again. She was married off to Lord Capulet before her brother ascended to the throne as a peace treaty. Janine wished she was married to a different man, but she couldn't change that without breaking the peace treaty that her parents, who are now dead, made and that kept her brother and her homeland safe from harm. She worried what was going to happen if Serenity ever went after Jonathan. She hoped her brother won't aid Jonathan if that time came.

CHAPTER SIXTY-SIX

AFTER TWO DAYS, Scott, Exotic, and Sasha finally docked in the port of China. Captain Mason walked up to Scott and his companions.

"Scott, you have forty-six hours to reboard with your sister and the rest of her companions, or you don't get on. Do I make myself clear? Or you will be stuck here from anywhere between a week to a month before I or another cruise ship returns here," said Captain Mason.

"Okay, I'll still take my chances to find my sister here in China. If we don't make it back, we will just have to lie low until the next ship comes around," said Scott.

"I figured you would say that. Good luck, Scott," said Captain Mason.

Scott did not say anything back to Captain Mason, hating the fact that his sister was friends with Captain Mason or in any type of relationship. Exotic and Sasha followed Scott off the ship to protect him and find their friends. They started searching China after they got off the ship, looking for any trace of Serenity, Yasha, Fang, or Cloud. As they travelled through China, Scott, Exotic, and Sasha got separated while searching for Serenity and the others. Sasha realized it first but couldn't care less at the moment. She was on the trail for Serenity, Fang, Yasha, and Cloud. She could tell the three of them were together for now.

Sasha travelled for another two hours and came upon an entrance to a cave where Serenity and the rest of their companions should be. She knew that Serenity will need to rest up, and it was daytime right now. So Serenity probably won't be leaving anytime soon with the sun up. Cloud got to his feet in a second sensing Sasha in the cave and picked up her scent. He went to the source of her scent. He found that Sasha stumbled upon their location.

"Sasha, why are you here alone?" asked Cloud, concerned with what's going on.

"I'm sorry, love, I just picked up your guy's scent and followed it here. Not paying attention, I got separated from the others," said Sasha.

"It's okay, love, we will meet up with the others later after Serenity gets some rest," said Cloud.

"Well, we should rest too while we have the time," said Sasha.

"Yes, we should. Any of the four of us will wake up if anyone gets too close to the cave," said Cloud. "Yasha and Fang woke up when your scent was close by, but I told them I would handle it," said Cloud.

"I bet you did just because you wanted to see me," said Sasha.

She then walked up close to the entrance and lay down and fell asleep to guard the cave. Cloud walked back a bit, about halfway between Sasha and the others, then got comfortable and fell back to sleep for more rest before nightfall.

***

Serenity started to get more strange dreams from Nikolai. She was pulled back into the past once again. This time he took her to a more recent event that involved Janine and Jonathan prior to her showing up in China as VHS captives again. She was inside the casino that Jonathan and Janine were working at. A group of vampire hunters just entered the casino. Janine spotted the hunters right away even though the hunters didn't spot her. Janine then calmly turned around and walked toward Jonathan to get him to leave the casino before he got caught by the vampire hunters. She saw that they were able to escape, there was a map of Iceland above their bed. She was thrown from the past to a possible future where Jonathan and she were getting into a fight, and he died at her hands, and the Capulet lands started to crumble to the ground. It showed her in pain lying on the ground, sensitive to the lands dying and making her ill in return. But Yasha came to her aid and made it so she couldn't feel the pain of the Capulet lands. The land was destroyed just by killing the lord where he had no heir to the throne.

Serenity was thrown back into the past this time, but further back, possibly before her father's time. She was no longer on earth in her dream but on a planet of ice and crystal, but there was no sun here. As she looked around, she noticed that all the lights were coming from the building. Serenity cupped her hands and put it into a hole in the ground. She noticed that it wasn't dry but wet; as she pulled her hand out, she noticed it was silver water. When she looked down, she saw what looked like earth. She was on a silver planet that looked down on the earth. She got scared thinking the planet she was seeing was habitable at one time even though she couldn't pinpoint it.

She saw the castle, and it was similar to one she saw in her vision of a future in the Ice and Crystal Land on earth. She wondered if there was a connection between the Ice and Crystal Land and this planet. She saw the lord talking to the lady, but what scared her was the language wasn't from earth, but she still understood it. As they talked, they said they would send their people to the land and stabilize a second type of land and home for their people, creating a new life for them. Right then she knew there were more than vampires that used more than one type of magic. They even mentioned making a royal family; they'd live on earth, and one day, the princess will rebuild her life and return home to some of her family and her people.

"Sweetheart, it will be okay. This will be your fate," said the spirit of her father, Nikolai Belikov.

"I don't know if I can do this," said Serenity.

"I know, sweetheart, only time will tell, so rest up," said Nikolai.

Nikolai did it again and comforted Serenity in her mind after showing her more of the vision.

CHAPTER SIXTY-SEVEN

SCOTT HAD BEEN traveling for about four hours alone trying to find the gang, again, he lost earlier by accident. Scott noticed a camp for an army. As he walked by, two of the day guards grabbed him.

"Let me go," screamed Scott.

General Jacob got curious of the commotion in the camp. General Jacob found the source of the screaming and fighting. He took a good look at the man his guards had. Scot had short green hair and silver highlights, green eyes, tan skin. He was wearing a black and green vest, a gray T-shirt, black and green jeans, black boots. General Jacob got between his man and the young man.

"Sir, I've come to believe you are Serenity's younger brother," said General Jacob.

"You know my sister Serenity?" asked Scott.

"Yes, she left quite a few hours ago with three men. I believe they went by Yasha, Fang, and Cloud," said General Jacob.

"That's good, they will keep her safe," said Scott.

"I hope you're right. There are some disturbing men after her," said General Jacob.

"Any chance you can describe the men to me?" asked Scott.

"Sure. They wear long black trench coats, black jeans, and steel-toed boats that are black as well. Their hair was tied back or very short. It also looked like they were carrying hidden weapons on them under the coat," said General Jacob.

"You definitely saw vampire hunters," said Scott.

Scott was worried about his sister now. He wished she would call him now to let him know she is safe, but he knew she won't call him in case anyone had found a way to tap either of their phones.

***

It was nightfall, and Serenity got up fully rested. Yasha woke up to her movement.

"Serenity, is everything okay?" asked Yasha.

"I just want to meet up with my brother and head to Iceland," said Serenity.

"Okay, well, let's wake up the others and split up, look for him, and meet up back at Captain Mason's ship by the end of the day," said Yasha.

"Sounds good to me," said Serenity.

Serenity went around the cave waking up Fang, Cloud, and Sasha. Sasha was the last she woke up since she was near the cave entrance. Cloud and Sasha woke up without Serenity touching; all she had to do was walk toward them at the entrance of the cave.

"Where are we going now?" asked Sasha.

"We are splitting up to go after Scott and Exotic," said Serenity.

"Are you crazy? You need protection," asked Sasha.

"Yes, Yasha, Fang, and I will take to the sky and try and find them. Cloud and you will stay on the ground and search for them as we make our way back to the port," said Serenity.

"Okay, understood," said Sasha.

Yasha grabbed Serenity and took to the sky to look for Exotic and Scott. Serenity let out her own wings to fly, and Yasha allowed her to fly. After an hour of flying, Serenity spotted Exotic resting in human form under a tree in a shaded place. Yasha and Serenity descended to the ground and landed next to her. Exotic woke up with them landing next to her. The breeze from their wings woke her.

"Yasha and Serenity, what brings you here?" asked Exotic.

"We are looking for you and Scott while heading back to the port. And can you fly? It will be quicker to get back to the ship," said Yasha.

"Yes, but wouldn't it be easier to walk?" asked Exotic.

"No, not with so many vampire hunters on the ground after Serenity," said Yasha.

"Okay, then, flying it is," said Exotic.

Yasha, Exotic, and Serenity took to the sky. Yasha was relieved that they didn't have to resort to walking back to the ship and look for Scott along the way. Serenity couldn't help it but watch the scenery pass them by as they were flying above China. Serenity loved being up high, unlike her brother Scott. Yasha kept looking from where they were heading to Serenity and Exotic, making sure he hadn't lost the girls and that they were still with him. They landed about a mile away from the port, knowing they still needed to run their cards to get back on the ship, but also knowing they needed to keep it so they aren't discovered as creatures or, as humans put it, demons. Serenity was walking on her own for now.

"Exotic, what's wrong? You look like you're worried about someone," said Serenity.

"Yeah, I am worried about Scott," said Serenity.

"Don't worry about too much about my brother. He can handle himself in a fight. Besides, I'm sure Cloud can find him easy enough. If not, Sasha knows my brother's scent and can pick up his trail," said Serenity, smiling.

"Okay, but you should rest once we get on the ship, Serenity," said Exotic.

Serenity nodded in agreement. They walked and got on the ship, hoping to eventually run into Scott. Serenity got on the ship and went to the infirmary to see the doctor on board. She knocked, unsure if the doctor was in there.

"Hello, Serenity, how may I help you?" asked the doctor.

"Yes, do you have any blood IVs? I need some blood," said Serenity.

"Are you feeling dizzy?" asked the doctor.

"No, but I've been in trouble with hunters again," said Serenity.

"Okay, lie down and get some rest. I'll set you up and get you some seasickness meds in you before we leave port," said the doctor.

The blood IV was out of the cold storage for her, and the doctor needed to talk to Captain Mason. The doctor needed to know how long before they leave the port so he can determine what type of seasickness pill she will need.

CHAPTER SIXTY-EIGHT

CLOUD AND SASHA were on their way back to the port and spotted Scott walking toward them.

"Hey, Scott, over here," called out Sasha.

Scott spun around in their direction. He then met him halfway.

"Cloud, do you know where my sister is?" asked Scott worriedly.

"Yeah, I believe back on the ship with Yasha and the others," said Cloud.

"What time is it now?" asked Scott worriedly.

"It's about 6:00 p.m. Why?" asked Cloud.

"Any chance we can make it back to the ship in an hour?" asked Scott.

"Yes, but you won't like it, Scott," said Cloud.

"You don't mean flying as close as we can then running the rest of the way?" asked Scott.

"Sasha, try and run ahead and see if you can stall Captain Mason at all, or see if they're still boarding so we have time to make it there," said Cloud.

"Will do, love," said Sasha.

"Cloud, don't even think it. I hate heights," said Scott.

"That's too bad, time's not on our side," said Cloud.

Cloud grabbed Scott and took to the sky before Scott could run off on him. Scott started fighting and resisting Cloud, wanting to be down on the ground.

"Damn it, Scott, stop being a child about this," Cloud yelled at Scott while in the air.

"Fine, just land soon. I want to be down," said Scott angrily.

Cloud ignored Scott's complaining, needing to focus to make it as close as possible to the port quickly so they can make a run for the reloading of the ship. Cloud clocked in a special spell to hide them in the air. He descended close to the port in a dark alleyway only about a twenty-minute walk to the ship.

CHAPTER SIXTY-NINE

JANINE WAS JUST getting up to start her night shift and was worried as hell about Serenity. She wondered if she even knew anything about the past or even the future possibilities. God, she hoped not the past; it was too horrifying, but she knew she couldn't protect Serenity from everything. Once she was ready for work and leaving the room, she cleared her mind of her worries. She had to be a 100 percent focused on the task at hand. Her husband didn't know what was on her mind these days. They hardly spoke when on the clock.

When they both were off the clock, they'd forget to talk about what was troubling her. Janine didn't want Jonathan to hurt Serenity. Royal vampire families were worse than the commoners on their children. If Jonathan wanted to, he could probably abuse Serenity and get away with it, since she was not his child. The court system hated getting involved in royal affairs. If one royal family hurt another, the court system would brush it off unless there was hard-core evidence. Nothing was fair in life among the royal families of vampires or other creatures. Janine wished Serenity would stay away and abandon the plan and hide in her real father's land.

At the port in China, Sasha made it to the ship, checked in with port authorities to reboard, then decided to try to make it to the engine room undetected by the crew that would try to stop her. She decided to use the cape Serenity left her back in the Hathaways' land. She made it, and she took the clock off and tucked it away in a place she could grab it and run if needed. She cut the power cord and shut down one of the engines and disconnected it for repairs in the engine room. While everyone in the engine room was in the dark, she sneaked back out and went to find Serenity. As she searched for Serenity, she found her fast asleep in the infirmary, hooked up to a blood IV drip. Sasha was guessing by the way Serenity was right now that she pushed herself when the VHs kidnapped her from the ship. Sasha lay at Serenity's feet on the bed and fell asleep.

CHAPTER SEVENTY

AN ENGINE CREW member ran to the captain's stateroom when he found they couldn't get power running or the engines to start; what was in perfect condition when they docked was now sabotaged. The crew member barged into the captain's stateroom.

"Captain Mason, sir, something went wrong. We can't start the engines," said the engine crew member.

"What they where clean when we docked two days ago, and when you guys did check an hour go when the port crew was assaying the ship," said Captain Mason, frustrated now.

Captain Mason called back the port maintenance crew to check the problem. While the men went over the footage of the engine room and the hallway that led to the engine room. The only thing they found was a shadow of a wolf in the engine room; nothing on who or what damaged the engines of the ship or power to the engine room. It took the maintenance crew an hour to reconnect everything and check to make sure everything was running smoothly. By the time they were done, Cloud and Scott made it back on board while the ship was still preparing to leave. Sasha sensed Cloud was back on board the ship and woke up and ran to him, leaving Serenity to rest. Cloud patted Sasha on the head since she was in wolf form in front of him. The ship started up, and the maintenance crew disembarked. Once everything was pulled away from the ship, they started to pull away from port and were heading to Iceland, and their final destination will be back to Russia.

***

Serenity was thrown back into the past once again; this time it was to Jonathan's past, which she may hate afterward. Jonathan was eighteen before he became lord. There was Jonathan, Janine, Irshrose, and Nikolai. Jonathan was dating Domka, Nikolai's twin sister. Jonathan and Domka decided to sneak off campus to an abandoned building. Two years later, she had a baby girl, and Jonathan took the baby and left Domka because she didn't give him what he wanted from her. Jonathan always was cruel and heartless toward women. Knowing it could happen to her and her mother. But she didn't plan on allowing him to touch her or her mother again. There was one thing in the world she couldn't forgive, and that was abuse. She'd taken enough of it from Jonathan as a child; she would not put up with it as an adult. She would stand up for herself and everyone she loved. She hoped Jonathan hadn't killed her mother yet or harmed Janine yet; if he did, she won't forgive him. She knew deep down Janine would die protecting her from Jonathan, if she had to make the choice; it pained her to think of the possible outcomes after she reunites all of them knowing the truth. All she wanted was a happy family. She wanted to be able to love Yasha freely, even though that was a far-fetched dream.

Serenity woke up when the day turned to night. Again, she was famished. But out of the blue, Yasha walked in the infirmary with a big plate of food.

"Is that for me?" asked Serenity, starving.

"Yes, love, eat up. You need everything you can get. We will be in Iceland by sunrise," said Yasha.

"Good, I want to talk to Janine," said Serenity.

"Why, love, have you been having strange dreams?" asked Yasha, worried.

"Yes, love, but I'll be okay. They're normally not about me. They are about my parents' past," said Serenity.

"Okay, just be careful. Knowing the past can be dangerous for you, love," said Yasha.

"I will as much as I can be," said Serenity.

She downed the rest of her food then got some rest, not sure if it would be day or night by the time they arrive in Iceland, at its port in a few hours.

CHAPTER SEVENTY-ONE

YASHA WOKE UP to the ship engines stopping. He noticed Serenity was still sound asleep and cuddled up close to him. Cloud walked in to the room unannounced.

"Cloud, can you wait? Serenity is still resting," asked Yasha.

"Because Iceland is doing a check, making sure everyone legally can enter before allowed off the ship," said Cloud.

"So why should that worry me?" asked Cloud.

"Because I don't think Sasha and Exotic have a passport to show they are allowed to enter," said Cloud.

"Well, I don't have one because I can pass as a pet," said Sasha.

"Fine, no talking and no reverting back to human form while we are here in Iceland," said Cloud.

"Fine, will do," said Sasha, annoyed.

A member of Iceland patrol knocked on the door where Serenity, Scott, Yasha, Fang, Exotic, and Sasha were meeting. Sasha reverted to wolf form before anyone opened the door. Cloud opened the door to the room.

"We need to see everyone's passport and pet registry for wolf," said the port officer.

They all showed their passports, and Serenity handed over her registration papers for the wolf as well.

"Miss Capulet, you are responsible to keep a leash and collar on the wolf in a crowded area, clear?" asked the por officer.

"Yes, sir, I understand the rules," said Serenity.

It took two hours before Captain Mason could enter the Iceland port.

"Welcome back to Iceland, Captain Mason. You here for your normal two-week stay?" asked the port manager.

"Yes, I'm taking a break before my next trip. Just make sure she's ready and loaded when I leave. If a woman by Serenity comes looking for me with a party before them, give me a call," said Captain Mason.

"Yes, sir, Captain Mason," said the port manager.

Captain Mason wished he could show Serenity some of the hot spots here in Iceland but knew that wasn't the reason she came here for. Lev went to his thinking place—the one place he could be true to himself even though it would probably never work out between him and Serenity.

Serenity and her companions just got off the ship, and even though Jonathan and Janine were one hundred miles away, Serenity picked up on Jonathan's aura.

"Serenity, do you have a clue where to start looking for them?" asked Yasha.

"Yep, and if we make it back in time, we can ship back with Captain Mason," said Serenity.

"One small problem: I'll have to take a separate ship home," said Yasha.

"Why, Yasha? I don't want to be without you," said Serenity.

"Sorry, love, your father shouldn't know about me yet, love," said Yasha.

"Fang is right, since we don't need a fight on foreign soil," said Cloud.

"So do you have to leave right now?" asked Serenity.

"No, not until we get close to your parents' work," said Yasha.

Serenity frowned, not wanting him to leave her pregnant. Yasha kissed her forehead and put his hand over his family pendant she was wearing.

"Serenity, don't forget, no matter where you are or how far away you are from me, I am always connected with you as long as you keep my pendant on you," said Yasha.

Serenity's eyes filled up with tears. Yasha wrapped his arms around her. He wished deeply that their families were allies. But they weren't since their fathers were bitter enemies. Cloud budged them to start moving; daytime would be creeping up on them, and they needed shelter. Serenity shouldn't be exposed to much sunlight; it could drain all her strength.

It took them two hours to find a place to stay. They made it in time so Serenity wasn't to exposed to the sun. They were staying in a cave. Serenity was curled up to Yasha to rest. Scott and Exotic were cuddling, and Fang was lying alone. Sasha was sleeping near the entrance being protective, and Cloud was sleeping halfway in to be a second-line defense against vampire hunters. If someone got past them, Scott and Exotic still stood between Serenity and Yasha before hunters could get their hands on her, but they would have to deal with a dragon who was deadly with breathing fire and a dhampir who was trained to keep enemies of vampires. Even if they made it to Serenity and Yasha, they still had to deal with Yasha and Fang. Fang, a falcon with deadly magic and weapon skills, and Yasha, an archangel who has dangerous magic and deadly skills with the sword.

It was almost nighttime when Sasha suddenly woke up by a clinging noise of a weapon hitting against each other, getting closer to the cave. She got up to focus on where the noise was coming from. When the man was in sight, he was 6'8" tall, had long black wavy hair, but some of it covered the left side of his face, so you couldn't see his eye. He had tan skin and silver eyes. He wore a long black trench coat, black pants, black boots, white shirt, and a red tie. He had a sword and rifle crossing each other on his back and two hand guns on each hip. Sasha noticed he was a hunter of some kind.

Serenity came outside recognizing the hunter and thought, *He is a legend back home.*

"Dmitr, why are you here in Iceland, and who is your target?" asked Serenity, knowing he wouldn't come this far unless his target escaped to Iceland.

"Well, well, a vampire princess can talk back unafraid," said Dmitr.

"Yes, I'm not afraid of fighting hunters," said Serenity.

"Well, unlike my comrades, I'm not here to fight the head of VHS asked me to bring you unharmed, preferably in your own free will," said Dmitr.

"When and where?" asked Serenity, cautious on saying she would go.

"Russia, and when you are able to return," said Dmitr.

"Give me three weeks and meet me at Fallower Café and Bakery at 7:00 p.m.," said Serenity.

"Well, okay, vampire princess Serenity, but if you are one minute late, I'll come looking for you," said Dmitr.

"Fine with me," said Serenity.

Dmitr left the area, leaving Serenity alone. Serenity and her companions had to meet up, with Janine and Jonathan staying here in Iceland.

CHAPTER SEVENTY-TWO

JANINE HAS BEEN in her new position for a week now. When she left the bar in the casino to do her other rounds, she spotted Serenity.

"Serenity, what are you doing here in Iceland, and how did you know to look here for us?" asked Janine.

"My new power," said Serenity.

"You should have stayed away, your father may not want you in our house now," said Janine.

"Mom can straighten everything out later. Besides, I know the truth. You and Jonathan aren't my actual parents. I'm not going to run away from danger anymore. I will face my fears and overcome them," said Serenity.

"You have changed a lot, young lady, since the carnival in America," said Janine.

"Yes, brother and the rest of my companions are waiting for us just beyond the forest," said Serenity.

"Well, I see you didn't travel alone then," said Janine.

"No, my companions wouldn't let me," said Serenity.

"That's good, sweetie," said Janine.

Janine vanished inside the casino. Serenity was relieved that Janine hasn't changed since they've been separated for almost a year. The only thing that has changed is she is now almost five months pregnant. She was so scared to tell them since Yasha is the father. She was happy that Yasha is the father. Serenity started to wonder what the unborn babies will look like. She was hoping that she was having twins of some sort. Serenity went outside to see Yasha one last time before Jonathan and Janine came out of the casino and they go home for good.

"Serenity, do you think you can handle me gone from your side for a week?" asked Yasha.

"Honestly, I don't think I can make it past loading of the ship, but I know if I really need you, you will create space in my room where we can be together for a while," said Serenity.

"Do you think you can try and handle it without me doing that, love?" asked Yasha.

"Yes, I can try, Yasha," said Serenity.

She gripped tightly his family pendant she was wearing. Yasha kissed her forehead then left, taking to the air. Fang also took off to avoid conflict with Lord Capulet. Serenity returned to just outside the casino to wait for Janine and Jonathan.

Inside, Janine went to Jonathan's work area to see if he was still working. Jonathan spotted his wife.

"Janine love, why are you here right now?" asked Jonathan panicky.

"Calm down, love, it's good news," said Janine.

"What's the good news that's got you smiling?" asked Jonathan.

"Serenity is here. We can go home now, love," said Janine.

Relief washed over Jonathan, and the desire to return home to his castle and lands.

"Let's go, Janine, I want our lives back to normal," said Jonathan.

"Okay, sounds good, love," said Janine.

Janine wondered if normal would be good or bad for Serenity. She didn't want to see Serenity getting hurt. Janine and Serenity walked into the manager's office side by side.

"Jonathan and Janine, what can I do for you?" asked the manager.

"We are quitting effective immediately," said Janine.

"Why? If I may ask?" asked the manager.

"We are returning back home to Russia," said Janine.

"Is there any chance I can change your minds?" asked the manager.

"No, there is no changing our minds," said Janine.

"Okay then, safe travels," said the manager.

Janine and Jonathan returned to their room and packed. They left their uniform in the room and only took what they brought with them. They then left the hotel room with a tip for the cleaning ladies and their room keys. A few minutes later, Janine and Jonathan came out with two suitcases, one for each of them. Serenity knew for now she needed to play the part of a loyal daughter even though she knew the truth.

"Mom and Dad, shall we go?" asked Serenity.

"Yes, sweetie, we should try to get as far as we possibly can before sunrise. Your father and you shouldn't be exposed to sunlight. It's unhealthy for you," said Janine.

"Janine, we will be fine if Serenity knows her sun-barrier magic," said Jonathan.

"Father, I couldn't and shouldn't use my magic too much right now," said Serenity.

"Serenity, are you saying you're pregnant without being married first?" asked Jonathan, pissed off.

"Yes, Father, I know it was wrong, but one thing led to another, and I had to mate with a man I didn't know well or love," said Serenity.

"Fine, we will go as far as we can before sunrise," said Jonathan.

"Father, I have friend that can fly or cover my skin from the sunlight," said Serenity.

"Why should we fly, where to, and who?" asked Jonathan.

"Because our ship back home leaves less than a week, and we need to make it back to the port before then," said Serenity.

"Lord Capulet, if you and Serenity are able to fly, I can keep the sun off your skins, and if I will carry Sasha, you carry Janine, and Exotic carries Scott, we can make it back to the port in time and safely," said Cloud.

"Fine, we can do it your way. I don't want anyone hurt or left behind. Serenity, can you even fly, sweetie? I've never seen you fly," asked Jonathan.

"Yes, Father, we can do it Cloud's way, and all of us will make it back to the port on time," said Serenity.

"Fine, Cloud, we will do it your way," said Lord Capulet.

CHAPTER SEVENTY-THREE

LEV RETURNED TO his ship four days early, having felt Serenity would return to the ship early for rest before he sails out. Serenity, Cloud, Exotic, and Jonathan landed as close to the port as possible with three of them carrying someone. They landed about an hour's walk away. They didn't want to make Serenity walk too far, but it was as close as they could manage to get to the port. Cloud spotted a hotel nearby.

"Serenity, do you still got a budget for a hotel so we all can get rest before continuing to the ship?" asked Cloud.

"Yes, we can get hotel rooms for all us for at least three days on money I got with us," said Serenity.

"Lord Capulet, can you agree to an eight-to-twelve-hour stay here so everyone gets rested up?" asked Cloud.

"Yes," said Lord Capulet.

Serenity paid for them all to stay in the hotel but in split-up rooms. She put Cloud, Sasha, and her in one room; Jonathan and Janine in another; and Scott and Exotic in another room. Exotic didn't trust Lord Capulet out of pure instinct. Cloud approached Exotic.

"Exotic, do you have a problem with Lord Capulet?" asked Cloud.

"Yes, but I'm not sure why. It's probably just my natural instinct kicking in," said Exotic.

"It's a good thing you don't. I'm not sure what Lord Capulet is capable of doing to Serenity. If we are lucky, tomorrow, when we get to the ship, Captain Mason will already be there," said Cloud.

They all got some rest before finishing the last stretch to the port. Serenity woke up after two hours of sleep and left her room without anyone knowing. She started walking back to the cruise ship by herself. Serenity knew they would meet her there, but she didn't want to be near

Jonathan more than she had to. Once she made it to the port, she was greeted by the port manager.

"Miss, I'm sorry, but none of the ships are boarding for two more days," said the port manager.

"I would like to see Captain Lev Mason and board his ship," said Serenity.

"What is your name? I'll call him. He is on his ship, just returned yesterday," said the port manager.

"My name is Serenity Irshrose Capulet," said Serenity.

"I'll just call him, let him know you are on your way. You may pass," said the port manager.

When Serenity reached Captain Mason's ship, she was greeted by the first mate.

"Welcome back, Miss Capulet," said the first mate.

"Is your captain in his quarters or the captain's stateroom?" asked Serenity.

"He is resting in his quarters. Would you like me to go get him?" asked the first mate.

"No, thank you. I know my way. I'll see myself to his quarters," said Serenity.

"As you wish, Miss Capulet. Just be warned, he's short-tempered if disturbed," said the first mate.

"I'll take my chances," said Serenity, walking away toward the captain's quarters.

Serenity went for Captain Mason's room to make sure she could get protection from Jonathan, not sure what that man may do to her. She went to knock on the door, but the door opened before she had a chance to.

"I have been expecting you, Princess Serenity," said Captain Mason.

"Can I please stay here until we take off?" asked Serenity.

"Anything for you, princess," said Captain Mason.

Serenity walked over to his bed and crashed from sneaking off on her companions, Jonathan, and Janine. She knew she could be in trouble without protection from Jonathan.

When night fell upon Iceland, Cloud and everyone else woke up in the hotel to find Serenity missing. They figured that Serenity went back to the ship ahead of them, unable to sleep. They knew if they stayed together and walked the rest of the way, they could make it by sunrise and follow Cloud's lead.

"Cloud, will Serenity be okay on her own?" asked Janine.

"Yes, she's safer on the ship than traveling with us," said Cloud.

Cloud was hoping his judgement was right about Lev. He didn't want to disappoint Lady Janine.

CHAPTER SEVENTY-FOUR

SERENITY WOKE UP to see Lev asleep next to her on the bed.
"Princess, are you hungry?" asked Captain Mason.

"Yes, I am," said Serenity.

"Okay, let me treat you to dinner then," said Captain Mason.

"Are you sure you don't need to stay with the ship?" asked Serenity.

"I don't have to be on the ship until we start boarding. It'll be fine," said Captain Mason.

"Okay, that sounds good to me," said Serenity.

Lev and Serenity left the ship and port while there was no one else supposed to be boarding until later that next day. So he planned to take her out for a late dinner just outside of the port. Serenity spotted a nice restaurant but not sure if Lev would approve going there. Lev was a middle-class worker, and the restaurant she chose was more for high-class people. Lev grabbed Serenity's hand and led her to the place she wanted to go for dinner.

"Come on, Serenity, I'll take you to the restaurant you are eyeing. It may be high-class, but only the best for you," said Lev.

Serenity was surprised at the way Lev was treating her.

"Captain Mason, you don't have to treat me to whatever I want," said Serenity.

"I know, but I want to," said Lev.

"Okay, we can do it your way," said Serenity.

"Thank you, Princess Serenity," said Lev.

Serenity smiled at him, happy to play along with his humoring nature. When Lev and Serenity got inside, they were seated right away. Serenity felt lucky; she always wanted try the high-class restaurants outside of Russia and see what types of food they offered.

It took Cloud and everyone else eight hours to walk back to the port. They still have close to another full four hours before the ship departs form the port. They were stopped by the port manager.

"Wait up, where do you think you all are going, and were is owner of the wolf?" asked the port manager.

"We would like to board Captain Mason's ship, and the owner should be on the ship," said Cloud.

"You are with Princess Serenity. You may board," said the port manager.

Everyone went to the room they were in before, except for Janine and Jonathan, who were assigned a room on the opposite end of the ship away from Serenity. Janine wanted to stay with her husband to make sure he kept his hands off of Serenity. She didn't trust him not to hurt her after finding out she is pregnant.

CHAPTER SEVENTY-FIVE

YASHA HAD BEEN on his own for almost forty-eight hours. In that time, he had made it back home in Russia. He walked through his family's castle and made it to his room without having to speak with his father. He crashed down on his bed exhausted from the flight home. The feeling of sleeping in bed now was unnatural without Serenity next to him. The last five months, he's been at her side ever since that night that they mated in Japan in the Hathaway lands that connected to the oracle temple. It pained him to leave her in the care of anther male, even though that male won't lay a hand on her the wrong way. None of her companions would be crazy enough to double-cross him. He has deeply fallen in love with Serenity, even though they weren't in love when he first mated her.

***

Lev and Serenity returned to the ship just before sunrise. Lev went to prepare the ship for departure. Serenity went to go see the doctor, to get blood IV so she can last until she gets back to Russia. She knew she needed to keep using her vampire form for a while longer, which required blood regularly. After setting up Serenity with the blood IV, the doctor decided not to leave the infirmary with a vulnerable vampire resting. He knew her secret of being an oracle and was quite shocked Yasha hadn't come by yet to see her. He normally couldn't stand leaving her alone.

EPILOGUE

JONATHAN WAS PREPARING their arrival at their home; he was going to have a long talk with Serenity. He hoped she hadn't gone and gotten pregnant by an enemy of the family. Jonathan didn't know that she knew the past and that Janine and he aren't her parents. He was hoping to keep Lord Belikov's death buried in the past and the fact that her mother, Irshrose, is his captive. He was hoping to keep all the unspeakable things he's done to the Belikov family. Jonathan wanted to keep Janine and Serenity as puppets. Jonathan doubted he could keep Serenity in check to go along with his plans and war game among the vampires. He was afraid she would make a move that would forever break his leash on her.

If he couldn't use Serenity anymore, he would have to dispose of her. But he knew his wife would not allow him to harm Serenity. So he would have to find a way to regain his control on her before it was too late. Jonathan went to leave the room before Janine grabbed his arm.

"Babe, come back to bed, it is still too early for you to be up and about," said Janine.

"Okay, just for you, I will," said Jonathan.

He couldn't afford to lose his grip on his wife. It's bad enough his grip on Serenity was slowly slipping away from him.

***

Serenity was being shown another part of the past by Nikolai Belikov. It was when her mother was still with him. Their oldest son was twelve years old, and their youngest daughter was four years old. One night, Lord Capulet showed up at the castle and busted into Lord Belikov's private study and stabbed him in the heart. Lord Belikov bled out until his body healed up on its own. Right then and there, Lord Capulet realized he couldn't turn Lord Belikov to ashes by his hand.

Serenity watched the nightmare that her real father's family was being destroyed by one man. As it played out, she watched as Lord Capulet was sealing her father in a tomb under the castle in a crystal so he couldn't ever interfere with Lord Capulet's plans.

When Serenity finally awoken, they had landed back home in Russia. She was asleep for three days straight on the cruise home. She disembarked the ship with Jonathan, Janine, and Scott to return back to their home. But she knew she had a lot of explaining to do later. But she planned to ride Icicle awhile first. So she whistled for Icicle, and Icicle came galloping right up to her. Serenity rode off into the darkness of the night, not to return home until sunrise.

SERENITY'S JOURNEY

New Beginning

C. L. Barrett

PROLOGUE

SERENITY HAS BEEN riding around on Icicle for hours now. It is time for her to be heading home and to face Jonathan, her adoptive father. She really doesn't want to have him punish her for falling in love with the enemy or, worse, kill the father of her unborn child/ren. So she sneaks into the castle and back to her room just before dawn, knowing Jonathan won't notice she returned home before nightfall; by then she should be able to leave or fight back, fully rested up.

Serenity is shown a vision of the future this time in her sleep. She sees herself surrounded by people that survived the fight and destruction of Lord Capulet's massacre of the royal family.

"Princess, will you lead us and save our lands, or what is left of it?" asked an elder.

"Yes, I will do whatever I can to restore this land back to its former glory," said Princess Serenity.

She knows this is what her real father, Lord Belikov, would want and would make him happy. Serenity starts to help the townspeople to rebuild what once was a beautiful kingdom. It once was the best place to live in all of Russia over twenty years ago. That was before Lord Capulet destroyed it. Serenity is crying in her sleep. She is sad that everything in the Land of Crystal and Ice was destroyed by Jonathan.

Serenity wakes up early, around 6:00 p.m. and looks at her personal calendar and remembers she needs to meet Dmitr in an hour at Follower Café and Bakery. Serenity gets dressed in commoner clothes and sits down and writes a letter and seals it with her royal seal. It reads,

> Dear Janine and Jonathan,
> Sorry I couldn't stick around for the talk later. I gotten an offer from Dmitr and meeting him. I'm going

to go meet him to find out more about it. I don't want to disappoint you but I need action in my life right now. Goodbye Janine. I will come home if I'm ever ready to return.

Sincerely,
Serenity Irshrose Capulet

Serenity neatly places the letter in front of the mirror next to her spare hairbrush. She packs light, knowing she will need a different set of clothes for hunting. She's not scared in her choice of a job. But she doesn't know how long she can do it before she needs to go on leave. Tonight is a new beginning of finding out who to trust and her real father's Land of Crystal and Ice.

CHAPTER ONE

IT'S 8:00 P.M. now, and both Janine and Jonathan are getting up for the night. Janine is worried that Serenity didn't come home last night. So while still in her nightgown, she goes to Serenity's room to check on her. When she first opens the door and walks in Serenity's room, she notices Serenity's bed has been used but was poorly put back together. She then checks Serenity's makeup stand, where she keeps her hairbrush. Janine notices a letter addressed to her and Jonathan written with care. When she reads it, she realizes Serenity cares for her and doesn't want her hurt by her leaving.

Janine tucked it into a drawer of the makeup stand to come back for it later. Janine makes up her mind to lie to her husband about Serenity. Janine returns to her husband and her chambers and starts crying as she walks in.

"Janine dear, what is the matter?" asks Jonathan.

"It's Serenity. She ran away because of…and never came home last night," says Janine.

"I'm sorry, love, we will find her, or she will come home on her own. She is a big girl now, Janine, let her go," says Jonathan.

"You insensitive bastard, she is our daughter. We raised her. She was four years old when you brought her home," says Janine.

"No, she only is an adopted daughter. I don't have to treat her the same way you do," says Jonathan with a grin.

"Why be so selfish? For it will get you killed one day, Jonathan," says Janine.

"I get what I want and don't care about anything else," says Jonathan.

***

Serenity notices Dmitr when he walks into the Fallower Café and Bakery.

"Dmitr, over here, quickly," says Serenity, loud enough so he can hear her over the noise of the café.

This café is only open at night; it's open from 5:00 p.m. until 3:00 a.m. every day. Dmitr eases his way in her direction. He knows it will be stupid to show fear in the café that mainly caters to vampires. Dmitr is not worried about showing fear where he doesn't show his emotions in front of others. After a minute, he reaches Serenity.

"Dmitr, I want to make one thing clear, and that is that I came here of my own free will," says Serenity before he can ask.

"Good, I'm glad you did," says Dmitr.

Serenity is able to show him a half smile.

"Dmitr, we should leave out the back now," says Serenity, sensing Lord Capulet's guards outside the café.

"Why? I just got here," asks Dmitr.

"Would you like a run-in with the royal guard that are after me?" asks Serenity seriously.

"You have a good point. Let's go," says Dmitr.

Serenity grabs her ribbon she keeps in her pocket and pulls her hair back. Dmitr has Serenity leave the café first since she is the target, and he is tall enough to keep her hidden from the guards. When they step outside, she senses more guards nearby.

"Dmitr, we have to split up. We will need to regroup after getting outside the Capulet lands," says Serenity.

Dmitr nods in agreement, knowing there is a higher risk of getting caught if he is with her. Dmitr can't risk being executed for hunting down a rogue princess. Dmitr starts retreating to an old abandoned warehouse that was used in a war against the Capulets as a hunter's base. It was a war his parents fought in when he was only a few years old. But he has a strange feeling that she doesn't belong to the Capulet family. He is positive that she isn't Janine's daughter. There is one question he still can't figure out yet, and that's who her parents are. Dmitr makes one last-minute decision that changes his location; he is going and headed to the Land of Crystal and Ice. Dmitr wants to know about Lord Belikov; he knows it's a silly idea since Lord Belikov has been dead for the last twenty years. Serenity looks too old to be his daughter, if he's been dead that long, it would mean Lord Capulet had her since she was at least four years old. Dmitr knows it's silly to think a dead man could possibly be Serenity's father. He knows that Serenity can't be controlled, but he is not sure what exactly she is.

It takes him two hours to walk to the Land of Crystal and Ice. Dmitr notices all of the villages and homes in one piece still. He wonders if everyone that survived the massacre still lives here. It is very possible that many generations live here from the past. One thing is for sure: this land can still become more advanced than anywhere else if it has the rightful ruler. All the buildings are made out of crystals and ice but not all the same colors. But out of all the palaces in the lands, the castle is the most magnificent. It is made from the rarest crystals and ice. The castle closes to one hundred stories tall. It goes out one hundred acres as well. They have a private garden out back of the castle. The garden is made out of rare flowers that only grow in a crystal and ice environment. They have a pool that's as big as a ballroom outside in the garden.

Dmitr goes inside the castle after thoroughly investigating outside the castle. When he enters the castle, he is greeted by head general Ace.

"Sir, this castle is off-limits to vampire hunters," says Head General Ace.

"I'm a vampire hunter, but I came here for information," says Dmitr.

"Fine, what kind of information are you after?" asks Head General Ace.

"I need to know what Lord Belikov looks like," says Dmitr.

"Why should I show you what he looks like or trust you?" asks Head General Ace.

"I'm going to meet a princess I am positive isn't lord Jonathan Capulet's daughter. My suspicions lead me here believing that she is Lord Nikolai Belikov's daughter," says Dmitr.

"Why should a vampire hunter like you be interested in a royal vampire and royal archangel?" asks Head General Ace.

"We want to recruit her as a vampire hunter and healer to help the fight to keep the peace between humans and vampires," says Dmitr.

"Well, I guess I can help you with who her real father is, Dmitr," says Head General Ace.

Head General Ace and Dmitr take a seat in two chairs that sit in a hallway where visitors take off their shoes. Dmitr doesn't have a clue what he is getting himself into and that Vampire Hunter Society was in the middle of this royal massacre.